THE ONLY LIVING BOY

ROBERT GRAHAM grew up around Belfast and lives with his wife and three children in Manchester. He teaches Creative Writing at Manchester Metropolitan University's Cheshire Faculty. He is the co-author, with Keith Baty, of *Elvis — The Novel* (The Do-Not Press, 1997). His short stories have appeared in a variety of magazines and anthologies and on Radio 4. He is the author of *How To Write Fiction (And Think About It)* (Palgrave, 2006) and co-author of *The Road To Somewhere: A Creative Writing Companion* (Palgrave, 2005) and *Everything You Need To Know About Creative Writing* (Continuum, 2007). He has written and directed over a dozen youth theatre productions. His first novel, *Holy Joe*, was published by Troubador in 2006.

Angela !
Happy reading —
and thanks for
coming .
Robert Graham

ROBERT GRAHAM
THE ONLY LIVING BOY

SALT

CAMBRIDGE

PUBLISHED BY SALT PUBLISHING
14a High Street, Fulbourn, Cambridge CB21 5DH United Kingdom

© Robert Graham, 2009

The right of Robert Graham to be identified as the
author of this work has been asserted by him in accordance
with Section 77 of the Copyright, Designs and Patents Act 1988.

First published 2009

Printed and bound in the United Kingdom by Lightning Source UK Ltd

Typeset in Swift 11 / 14

ISBN 978 1 84471 574 9 paperback

Salt Publishing Ltd gratefully acknowledges
the financial assistance of Arts Council England

1 3 5 7 9 8 6 4 2

CONTENTS

THE ONLY LIVING BOY

WILL AND I and his sister Elaine, who was seventeen, were in the back seats of the camper van and when it crested the hill, Uncle Geoff's MGB GT was parked on the grass outside the cottage.

The front door admitted straight onto the living room, which had a three-piece suite covered in faded flowery chintz, a dining table with an oilcloth over it and an open fire with a kettle on an iron stand that you could swing over the flames.

'Just the same,' Will said and when I turned I saw he was carrying a record player and some records.

'Where'd they come from?' I asked.

'Elaine's.'

'Let's see.'

He gave me the LPs. There were four of them. *Bridge Over Troubled Water*, which everyone in the world owned a copy of; *Songs From A Room*; Bread's *On The Waters*, and *America* by, well, America.

I had wondered sometimes why Will got to bring a friend on holiday and Elaine didn't. If I had asked him about it he would have said it was because she had no friends, but I never asked. It turned out Elaine did have a friend and she was arriving on Monday. She was called Libby.

We were in the middle of a game of Monopoly, the three of us. The Simon & Garfunkel LP was playing. Elaine was cautious and hung on to her cash to cover any large rent demands she ran into, which was what had just happened: £600 for two houses on Will's Mayfair.

'Tee-hee-hee,' Will went.

'Don't gloat,' Elaine snapped, shuffling banknotes. 'Not a problem, as it happens.'

Paul Simon was declaring that there were times when he was so lonesome he took some comfort with the whores on 7th Avenue.

'What a pseud,' Will scoffed. 'He couldn't just go to the whores because he was feeling horny.'

'In fact,' I said, ' "Feeling Horny" was the original title of "Feeling Groovy". But they had to clean it up for radio.'

Later, 'The Only Living Boy In New York' played and the chorus — *So here I am, the only living boy in New York* — came in like a force 9 gale and knocked me sideways.

'What age is your friend?' I asked Elaine.

'Libby?' she said, like this was an unusual thing to ask. 'Seventeen.'

At breakfast that first Sunday, Uncle Geoff asked us if we wanted to take a turn at the wheel of the MG. Elaine was included in the invitation, but she didn't seem interested. Perhaps she thought driving cars was boys' stuff.

Outside, the sunlight was clear and airy and the sky as wide as any continent.

'You drive, Mark,' Uncle Geoff said. 'Visitors first, eh?' He opened the driver's door and ducked in to slide the key in the ignition. Rather than squeeze into the rear bench seat, Will opted to hang around on the beach until it was his turn. I glanced at him, but he wouldn't look me in the eye. While he trudged over the marram grass to the sands below, I lowered myself into the driver's seat. I was tall, and could have done with a shoehorn.

Once I was installed, it felt more like being in a cockpit than a car. I studied the array of chrome-ringed dials on the black instrument panel, patted the steering wheel and swung the gear lever from side to side. I looked across when Uncle Geoff appeared in the passenger seat and he beamed back at me.

'Engage the clutch,' he said. 'And move through the gears. That's right.' He asked me to put the gear lever back into neutral and then told me to switch on the engine. It turned over with a cough and settled into a warm, throaty sound.

I looked at Uncle Geoff, who nodded. I engaged first, gingerly released the clutch and set off, the engine revving as I progressed through the gears until it reached a sweet roar at thirty miles an hour. Through the windscreen, the pale strand swept towards me.

'Like it?' Uncle Geoff asked.

'I love it,' I said and gently put my foot down.

Monday morning, the sun had gone and the sky was washed over with grey. We were back on the beach with the MG, Will first this time. When my turn came, a mizzle began. Soon, enough raindrops were pattering on the windscreen for Uncle Geoff to tell me to put on the wipers. Up where the lane from the road comes down to the beach, I was turning the car through a circle to go back when an orange Maxi drove onto the sands and turned with me. Between the sweeps of the wipers, I saw a girl in the passenger seat, misted by the condensation on her window. For a moment or two after I straightened to head for the cottage we drove along side by side. The Maxi's passenger seat window was parallel with my side window and I looked over to see this girl with long blonde hair looking back at me. Her face was expressionless and in a few seconds she looked away.

When I drove up and parked behind the camper van and the Maxi, Uncle Geoff jumped out and pumped Libby's father's hand. 'No problems finding us?' he asked.

'What a lovely spot,' the other man said and laughed. 'Talk about getting away from it all.'

Libby was standing beside her father. She was tall and wore a strap-top, jeans and desert boots. Will was looking at her and I was looking at her, but she carefully avoided looking back. The five of us went up the path to the cottage, scrunching the rounded pebbles beneath our feet. I studied a pair of maracas hanging from one of the belt loops at the back of Libby's jeans.

As we came through the door, Elaine went 'Oh!' and jumped up from the sofa. She said, 'Hi' to Libby, laughed in a nervy way and crossed the room to link arms with her friend. 'Come on,' she said. 'I'll show you where we're sleeping.'

That afternoon, we went and played hopscotch on the sand. Libby was a sure shot and flew through the squares unstoppably. When she landed her stone in square ten, watching her hop up to it—one foot, two feet, one foot and so on— was all pleasure. She came back at twice the speed, hurtling towards Will. When she sailed through square one and home, Will caught her.

'What're you doing?' she asked, stepping away from him.

'Catching you.'

'I wasn't falling.'

Later, we changed into our swimming gear and went over

to the strand. Unlike Elaine, Libby wore a bikini. Elaine was smaller and softly curved, but Libby was long and slim, elegant. She jumped over the waves until she was up to her hips in the water, dived forward and began to swim. She seemed to be going for the horizon.

Will's face was screwed up. 'Who goes into the sea to swim?'

I nodded in her direction. 'Libby.'

When we went back to the cottage, Elaine offered to make everybody tea and scones. Will and I sat on the sofa and eavesdropped on the girls in the kitchen.

'Should we put on some music?' I murmured to Will.

'No,' he said, with an ear cocked toward the kitchen, where Elaine was now saying that she wanted to go to university and then get a job working for the government. 'Okay,' Will said.

I slid the Leonard Cohen LP from its paper slip case and popped it onto the turntable. As the needle crackled round the run-in strip before the first song, I flipped the card sleeve over and studied the photograph there: a woman, a good-looking woman, sitting at a table in nothing but a white towel.

Will stared at the door into the kitchen. 'She didn't like me catching her,' he said.

The sun woke me quite early on Tuesday morning and I heard a sound I recognised, the *klok-klok* of the maracas. I eased myself out from under the sheet and grabbed my clothes from the chair.

Libby was by the sink in the kitchen, drinking water from a glass. She looked over her shoulder at me.

'You're up early,' I said.

'So are you.'

'Going out?'

She nodded, slung the water and rinsed the glass. She gave me a smile and went out the back door. I followed and speeded up to walk along beside her.

'You're going out, too?' she said. On her belt loop, the maracas knocked against each other.

'Well—d'you mind having company?'

'I'll tell you when we get back.'

She was wearing clean, white Dunlop tennis shoes that looked smart with their green lining, but once we were on the sand, she took them off and walked barefoot. The light was fresh and new as we marched along. After half an hour we walked out on this little headland—just a sprinkling of black rocks protruding from the coast—and sat down.

'What'll you do when you leave school next year?' I said.

'Go to a Greek island and be a writer like that woman on the back of Elaine's Leonard Cohen LP.'

I had always taken the glamorous woman in the towel as the writer's girlfriend—not a writer. I just guessed that if you became a famous writer like Leonard Cohen your reward would be a beautiful blonde, tan in a white towel. But she was sitting at a typewriter.

'Aren't you going to university then?' I asked.

She looked at me, her blue eyes sparkling. 'Why would I do that?'

I asked her what she liked reading and she ran off a list: Lawrence, Hardy, Huxley, and Donleavy. I said I liked getting Penguin books because they matched. Even if the spines were different colours—orange, grey or green— they all had the same little Penguin. 'I'd like to go to Greece and have a girlfriend like that woman in the towel,' I said.

She laughed. 'You want to collect your paperbacks and I

don't want to have any possessions. I'm an absolutist, you see.'

I tried to think what an absolutist might be. 'You mean you do things to extremes?'

'Yes,' she said, stood up and set off.

On Wednesday, Uncle Geoff and Auntie Anne took Elaine up to Belfast to see a consultant about the cartilage in her knee.

Libby and I were reading in the garden. We sat on aluminium deck chairs. Will walked past us a couple of times without saying anything. Then he was standing in front of us dangling a set of keys—the MG keys.

'Want to take a spin to Newcastle and get an ice cream?' he asked.

'With an underage driver?' Libby said.

'Scared?' he said.

She wouldn't be, I thought; she's an absolutist.

'Okay,' Libby said and stood up. 'Let's go.'

Will drove. Libby sat in the passenger seat and I hunched up on the bench seat behind them. We were driving round Dundrum Bay when the engine died. I could see Will turn the ignition and I heard a dull click.

'What is it?' I said.

He grimaced. 'It's stalled.'

We were stationary at the side of the road. Will kept turning the key, but all he got was the same flat click. We got out and stood on the grass verge. Will kicked one of the tyres. Libby was carrying a small, powder blue handbag on a long strap, which she now lifted over her head so that the strap ran from one shoulder to the opposite hip. She didn't say anything.

A police car came round the bend behind us.

'Oh great,' Will said.

The police officer who emerged had a country look about him. The bulbous toecaps of his lace-up boots gleamed in the sunlight.

'In bother, youngsters?' he said.

Will was frozen to the spot.

'Who's the driver of this wee car?' the officer asked.

I watched Will's mouth drop open like an attic trapdoor. A season came and went and then Libby said, 'I am.'

'Would you just give me a wee look at your licence there, dear?'

Of course. Libby was seventeen. Why wouldn't she have passed her test?

The officer studied the licence, nodded and returned it to her. He got Libby into the driver's seat and explained a jump-start to her. He told Will and me that we would push. 'I can't afford to be annoying my lungs,' he said.

We leaned on a wing each and shoved the MG and it sped up as the road dipped and then the policeman bellowed out, 'Now!' The car jerked, the engine kicked in and Libby shot away from us and we almost ended up facedown on the tarmac. A hundred yards further on, she stopped and revved the engine. Before we knew it, the police car was driving past us. He bipped his horn as he overtook the MG and was gone.

At that moment, the MG took off again and, like the police car before it, disappeared around the bend.

Will looked at me, wide-eyed, and gasped. 'Can you believe that?' he said.

'Hey!' Will screamed and gave chase. 'Hey!'

He was wasting his time. She wouldn't be waiting for us further up the road. She was an absolutist; she did things to extremes.

The world was suddenly empty. I looked at the gorse bushes down by the shoreline, and, across the bay, at the blue Mourne Mountains. I'd like to be able to tell you that I said to myself, 'So here I am, the only living boy in New York.'

FRUIT OR VEGETABLE?

MARTHA SLICES TOMATOES over Shreddies for Molly's break-fast. Sarah is opening the post: a Racing Green catalogue, a Norweb Energi statement, a card from her Dad containing an avalanche of detail on a garden centre she already knows too much about, and a prayer-newsletter from the Weirs, a family from church who are mission partners in China, which she is about to open, when Martha distracts her.

'But we did fruit and vegetables in school this week, and Mrs Robinson definitely said tomatoes were a fruit. Really, Mummy.'

Sarah's mind drifts away from tomatoes and the morning post to settle on other things. She is thinking about Naomi, who died over a month ago, and when she thinks of Naomi she misses the maternal attentions of the older woman, which makes her sad. She also compares her own devotion to God to Naomi's, which makes her feel bad.

This morning, she sees this coming and goes to look for Molly instead. What she finds is her two-year-old singing on the stairs, drawing squiggles on the wallpaper with her Dad's antique Parker Duofold.

'You're a naughty girl.'

Molly wails as Sarah lifts her, marches back to the kitchen and plants her in her high chair.

'Agghh!' she groans, when her hand comes to Molly's bot-tom. 'You're wet. I'm sick of these leaking nappies.'

The roads they flow through on their way to the retail park

are almost free of traffic: this side of ten on a Saturday morning, anyone with any sense is in bed, enjoying a mug of tea, or—if they're really lucky—asleep. Sarah and Joe sit in stiff silence and look everywhere but at each other. Rain is drilling down on the sunroof.

They go to Children's World, where the aisles are imposing and long and the banks of shelves are ravines of garish colour. She can't help thinking that there are better ways to spend a Saturday morning than in a retail park. The way she sees herself is dutiful, but sometimes the temptation to escape her duties feels overwhelming.

Years ago, in another, single, life, a Saturday might have meant Scafell, Edale or Llanberis. It meant getting out of the jammed city and feeling free amongst the leaves and lambs and hills. Single life and years ago are very appealing this morning. Ever since Naomi's death, she has been feeling bad about her own life. Jesus was so apparent in Naomi and, compared to Sarah's, her priorities were so uncluttered.

Martha says, 'Mummy? Maybe it would work if we had tomatoes in fruit salad?'

'No.'

'But it's a fruit.'

'It might be a fruit, but it always gets treated like a vegetable.'

'Well, that's not fair, then, is it?'

Sarah thinks Martha gets her stubbornness from Joe. She wishes Joe would deal with it now. She wishes Joe would disappear off the face of the earth now.

She loves her children, but wonders if being a mother has to involve all the soul-numbing experiences that it seems to: shopping, cooking, a torturous relationship with the washing machine and consumer adventures like this trip to a retail park. In terms of living out the Christian message, her life seems a far cry from Naomi's, who was unencumbered by husband or children.

'Oh well, at least they're practical.'

'What?' Joe snaps.

She knows she has been wrong-footed here: she has said something in the middle of a train of thought, which always irritates Joe. Because she has been put on the defensive, she feels constrained to speak to him. 'Retail parks. They may be gross, but you can get a lot of stuff for children all in one spot.'

'I hate them.'

'Well I do, too.' The way he takes the aesthetic high ground like this makes her mad. Anyone would think he was the only person with any taste at all. She looks at him, at his dark, greying hair and his black spectacle frames, and she feels gloomy. 'But you don't have to like them to see that they're practical.'

'They're practical, and I hate them.'

Frustrated with not being able to find what she's looking for, Sarah leaves Joe and the girls in the play area.

As she strides down the aisle labelled 'Arts & Crafts', she snatches the bobble off the back of her head, sweeps the hair with both hands into a tighter, neater bunch and, holding it gathered in her left hand, twists the bobble round and round it with her right.

Last night, they visited a new colleague of Joe's—a new, glamorous, young colleague of Joe's. Including Charlotte, their hostess, there were seven of them for a meal. Not exactly a meal; something more casual than that. True, there was summer pudding afterwards, but the preamble was a desultory smattering of choice, but inadequate, items: smoked salmon canapés, Stilton and Bath Olivers, something with anchovies.

Right in front of Sarah, Charlotte told Joe his voice was like honeycomb. 'Honestly. You should be on the radio.'

Joe raised his eyebrows and looked helpless.

Charlotte said, 'I've always been a sucker for gentle voices.'

Joe replied, 'What can I say?'

You could try telling her to bog off, Sarah thought, because the light of your life is sitting listening to this Gold Blend smarm. But, always a sucker for anyone who appeared to like him, Joe allowed himself to be led by the nose. Charlotte laughed at even the hint of wit and he lapped it up.

Most shameful of all for Sarah was when she complimented Charlotte on the tidiness of her house, nine parts Habitat to one part Japanese minimalism—and flawless.

'I have a woman who comes and does, twice a week.'

Joe said, 'We could do with that: a woman to come and do.'

'There's no need,' Sarah said. 'You've got a woman who stays and keeps on doing—me.'

The intention was to shame Joe in front of this slinky poppet, but it blew up in her own face.

'Mmm,' Charlotte said, throbbing in Joe's direction, 'I think I'd be the same if I had a nice, squeezy man. I'd just pamper him like a pussycat.'

Not long afterwards, Sarah and Joe left.

The assumption that everything to do with home and children is her responsibility makes her mad. All right, he might always get up first with the girls and more often than not give them breakfast. He might have changed a respectable number, if not his fair share, of nappies. He might take it in turn with her to either bath them or read the bedtime stories. But she is infuriated by the ever-present implication that because she only works part-time, she must be the principal homemaker and he nothing more than her naturally part-time assistant. It's being dutiful that has landed her in this position.

'I'm sick of it,' she mutters.

Sarah is looking for three items: a play-table for Molly's second birthday, a tapestry kit for her niece's sixth and something or other for the third birthday of one of Molly's little friends at her childminder's. The trouble is, there are too many products to choose from. This urban retail park has too many shops. And there are too many people out this morning, trying to make themselves happy by buying things they think they need.

She is beginning to despair not only of finding the presents she seeks, but also of doing anything satisfactory today at all. Something hits her behind the knee. She experiences a flash of adrenaline and, twisting round, comes face to face with a boy in a Buzz Lightyear track suit—*To Infinity And Beyond!* it says. He's maybe six or seven and she sees that he has kicked a football at her.

A man's voice calls, 'Sorry, love,' and when she looks in its direction she realises that this father and son are entertaining themselves by kicking a Children's World ball up and down the aisles.

She pulls a tight-lipped smile in response to the father.

'Aw 'ey, cheer up, love,' he goes.

Sarah flounces off in search of plastic furniture, the man's voice following her: 'Worse things happen at sea, pet, eh?'

'This,' Joe says, indicating the toddler-sized table between them and the shin-height chairs on which they are doubled up, 'is nonsense.'

Sarah doesn't want to discuss anything with Joe just now. As they were undressing for bed last night, Joe said, 'Charlotte flirts with everyone. It doesn't mean anything.'

'You don't have to put up with it, though. You don't have to accept it like a birthday treat.'

'You're too extreme about everything, faith included,' he

said and she failed to come up with a response. This remark has been needling her ever since.

But now, in spite of herself, she says, 'Sorry?'

'It's nonsense. I just hate the idea that having kids seems to condemn you to a life of consumerist mediocrity.'

Molly breaks off from sucking orange up her straw and points at Joe's cinnamon doughnut and says, 'Take.'

'That's right, sweetheart: cake. Daddy's cake. Maybe Daddy will break you off a piece of it.'

'Yeah!' Molly says, her mouth and eyes wide open in excitement.

'But as lives of consumerist mediocrity go,' Sarah says, feeling pleased with herself as she revises a Woody Allen quip, 'it's one of the best.'

Joe breaks the rest of his doughnut into pieces for Molly.

'Anyway,' Sarah says, suddenly angry, 'you always think you were so sharp and free before we had a family—before you were married, probably. But isn't mooching in Waterstone's just another form of the same thing?'

'No. Mooching in Waterstone's is a sublime experience.'

'It's still people thinking that they can find something to buy that'll make their lives better.'

Joe looks up to the ceiling and around the McDonald's and sighs. 'You're just in a bad mood this morning.'

Sarah gasps. 'I'm in a bad mood!'

'Yes, and all over nothing.'

'Oh, I wouldn't say Charlotte last night was nothing.'

'But why am I suffering today for what Charlotte is alleged to have done last night?'

On the way home, they stop at Beech Road, and Joe and Molly go to the Italian deli and buy a ciabatta, while Sarah and Martha pick up the latest issue of *Noddy* from the newsagents.

Sarah and Martha get back to the car first.

While Martha reads her comic, Sarah looks through the windscreen at all the twenty-somethings going about their Saturday morning business. They wear lime and orange and purple. Most of the men have goatees and most of the women wear slightly flared trousers with chunky, thick-heeled shoes. They mount the steps to The Lead Station for Czech lager and mozzarella salad or a latte. They emerge from Truth with their hair cut shaggy and feathered.

And then Joe and Martha are crossing the road and she thinks how fashionless he looks in comparison to the young singles she has been studying. If he, like her, has been looking around Beech Road, she believes he will have been thinking how footloose and unfettered, how young everyone here looks. And consequently, he will be feeling burdened, yoked and old.

'Smell this,' Joe says, when he has belted Molly into her car seat and is plumping himself down beside Sarah.

'Smells like freshly baked bread.'

'I know. Great, isn't it?'

'Is it? You seem to have cheered up very suddenly.'

'It's being amongst the beautiful people here.' He gestures out the windscreen. 'Makes me glad to be settled down and not have to impress some babe.'

'Really?'

'Really.' He turns to face Sarah. 'I've found my babe and moved onto the next phase: bringing up babies.'

Something heavy and tasting of metal sinks inside her.

Joe looks at her and says, 'What?'

'Right. So you can tick me off your list.'

'That's a bit twisted.'

She flips the door handle and swings her legs out. 'Drop dead.'

She goes to a florist's. She buys pink carnations because they last well, because at this time of year there isn't much choice and because she isn't thinking about what she's doing. By the time she emerges gripping the wrapped flowers, she is stiff with anger; she is cold stone, walking.

'Well,' she says to Joe, as she throws herself down on the passenger seat, 'are you going to apologise to me?'

'What?'

Martha and Molly come to attention like alert terriers.

'You heard.'

'Why would I do that?'

'Because you get it all your own way. You get a life at work, and at church, that I hardly even glimpse.'

'What are you talking about?'

'You. I'm talking about you. I'm sick of you being so self-contained and I'm sick of the way you just get on with your own precious priorities while I'm left to do put seven loads a week through the washing machine—'

'What have my priorities go to do with the bloody washing machine?'

'Nothing. That's just it. You just get on with the things you want to achieve. When do I ever get to achieve anything? When do I ever do anything I really want to do? All I get is a day that goes round the same and a week that goes round the same and it's all cooking and cleaning and hanging washing on the radiators and taking it off again and on and on. I can't remember the last time I was able to do something that was just for me.'

'But it's the same for me, practically. It's the same for any-one—'

'It's not the same for you!' She stabs the air in front of her with her finger to punctuate the word 'not'. 'You escape from us five days a week and most nights as soon as the children are in bed, you're upstairs farting about with your computer.'

'You're free to do what you want once the children are in bed, too. Besides, when I'm escaping from you to work and most of the time I spend on the computer too, I'm earning two thirds of our income. If you had your way, I'd spend all my time with you, I'd be your full-time assistant helping you run the family—but we wouldn't have any money to run it with.'

'Nonsense.' She flicks a commanding hand at him. 'Start the car, will you?'

'What's your rush to get home? Why can't we finish the argument here?'

'I'm not going home, that's the rush. If I did what I really want, none of you would ever see me again. I'd just be up and gone and leave you to sort yourselves out. But since I'm a slave to duty, you can just drive me where I want to go.'

'I don't know what all this is about.'

'Just drive.'

'Where to?'

'Drive and I'll tell you.'

As the car moves off, she turns around. Martha and Molly are sitting very still, their eyes like saucers.

'Mummy needs a little time on her own. You'll be all right with Daddy, pets, won't you?'

Molly nods.

Martha says, 'Are you going to be long?'

Sarah sighs and says, 'I don't know.' She sees they are passing Chorlton Park and orders Joe to stop, which he does, in silence.

Sarah opens her door, then turns to face Joe. 'And I'm really annoyed about you saying that I'm too extreme about everything, faith included.'

'What?'

'Last night, when we got back from Charlotte's.'

'You shouldn't take everything I say to heart.'

'Maybe if you were a little more extreme about your faith we wouldn't be having this argument.'

And she's out on the street and the door slams hard behind her. She marches towards the park gates, wading through the thick air, brandishing the carnations like a machete.

'Sarah!' she hears. 'Sarah!'

She slows and turns. The passenger seat window has been wound down and Joe is leaning across, his face flushed with anger or physical effort—she doesn't care which. He has stopped calling her name.

She stares at him and tells him, 'Later.'

Inside Chorlton Park, she launches herself across the empty football pitches. As she advances, she turns her anger to her scuffed Doc Martens and wonders when she will get a new pair of shoes. The fleecy she's wearing she's owned since well before she was married. She dearly wishes she had £500 to spend on clothes. She would like, in fact, a whole new wardrobe. The sum of £500 is only a nod to the reality of their finances and £500, she knows as she's thinking it, is impossible.

Out the other side of the park, she crosses Mauldeth Road and goes up Nell Lane, where she soon reaches Southern Cemetery. She is still shouldering a sackful of woes. Apart from the thing with Charlotte, of course, and all the domestic injustices she feels and the duties her dutifulness compels her to take care of, apart from Joe being a man and simply being Joe, there is the sense she has of having lost control of her life. She has collected too many responsibilities and her life now has a relentless momentum she feels powerless to alter. She could emulate the heroine of any of the Anne Tyler novels she loves and just up-sticks and start all over again. But the temptation, though powerful, wouldn't get her anywhere. The last Anne Tyler she read had a protagonist who threw up her family and started over only to duplicate her old life in her new one.

Here, among the graves and headstones of a couple of centuries, she has an appealing fantasy of death. After all, the only real escape is to the next world, where no tear will fall. But the shine goes off this daydream in seconds because she knows she couldn't bear to leave her girls to the mercies of anybody other than herself—even their father. What, she thinks, is a father's love compared to a mother's? Something, but not nearly enough.

She has gone through a transition now from anger to anxiety and one of the things that springs up to worry her is the possibility that she may have missed her calling—that God asked and she was unwilling or maybe not even tuned in enough to hear him. If true, that would have been Joe's fault, too. How much more effective she could have been as a single Christian. She is flooded with hatred for Joe and almost wishes him off the earth. Bitterness and resentment engulf her in a black, airless cloud.

She remembers something she once heard in a sermon: that often in relationships you have to force yourself to forgive; you have to breathe out forgiveness. And the preacher had modelled it by forcing a gust of breath out of himself to demonstrate. It was, he said, an act of will. You have to breathe out forgiveness. It is the last thing she feels like.

Naomi lies in a family plot in the old part of Southern Cemetery. As yet, there's no indication on the headstone that she has been buried there. Her father, the headstone says, was BELOVED HUSBAND AND DEVOTED FATHER; her mother, simply

LOVING WIFE. The fresh, red soil and the gravediggers' planks stacked nearby are the only traces of Naomi's burial.

Sarah stands for a moment, holding the carnations and reflecting.

At one time, years ago, they were in the same home group, where Naomi mothered Sarah and the other women. She remembers Naomi in the hospice, disappearing before their very eyes. She thinks of the fruit bushes Naomi gave her—redcurrant, raspberry and gooseberry. She remembers how Naomi divided her possessions amongst her friends at church, every item allotted to a specific individual—a sewing machine, suitcases, a radio-cassette, winter and summer coats, pewter vases and Toby jugs, a brass hearth set.

Suddenly Sarah is weeping freely, weeping and sobbing. The tears run into her mouth, the curtains sweep back off her heart, baring its tender surfaces to the sharp air of the open world. How, buried beneath her husband and children, will she ever grow to be the equal of Naomi? Can Jesus ever be as real to her as he clearly was to Naomi?

Sarah takes out her handkerchief and blows her nose noisily. The eruption of sound reminds her of Molly sucking orange up her straw in McDonald's and she melts at the mental image of her daughter. As she cries, as pained noises squeeze out of her, she sees that her heart is soft and not hard, that she loves her children more than she resents her circumstances. Truth is, she adores her children and thus she has a purpose in life—a calling, perhaps.

She inhales the air around her deeply and, finally, out loud to her husband wherever he is by now, she declares, 'I forgive you.'

As she wipes the tears off her cheeks and relishes the sudden, fresh rawness in her heart, she thinks that life—she hopes that life—is long. There may be time to grow more like

Naomi and time for fuller service to God. There may be time to be both mother and missionary. She resolves not to mix up God's timing with real seconds-and-hours time.

At home, Joe has made soup, which the family eats in a lighter, brighter mood.

'Red,' Molly says, pushing fragments of bread into her mouth and pointing at the soup.

'It's more orange, really,' Joe says.

'Monge-uh.'

'That's right.'

Sarah finds now that the prospect of breathing out is no longer so daunting. She draws in breath and lets it out again, willing continued forgiveness.

Martha turns to Joe and asks what's in the soup.

'Tomatoes—'

'So it's fruit soup?'

'Well—'

'Let's say fruit and vegetable,' Sarah says, and Martha seems happy with that.

CELEBRITY BLESSINGS

THE FIRST TIME I saw Raymond Carver was in Safeway. I knew it was him and I wasn't really surprised. Living in Chorlton, you get used to people turning up in Safeway. I've seen Una Stubbs, Vic Reeves, Julie Goodyear and Mick Hucknall in there. I passed this close to Ryan Giggs once. We could have chatted, if I'd been at all interested. 'Life's too short for sport,' I've been known to quip. And there you have it in a nutshell. Life's too short, full stop. Which brings us neatly back to Raymond Carver.

He was considering buying some Haagen-Dazs ice cream. He was wearing a brown Donegal tweed jacket, with a cream button-down Oxford, plain knit tie, Timberland shoes and beige flannels. Just as I recognised him he happened to look up and meet my glance. His eyes were blue, his expression gentle and open. I didn't know where to put myself. I mean, Julie Goodyear was easy; I never watch *Coronation Street*. But Raymond Carver. Here I am trying to write short stories and who do I walk into in the aisle between ice cream and TV dinners? Only the most feted English language short story writer of the past fifty years, that's all.

The first thing I read about Carver was that he only ever attempted to write what he knew he could finish in one sitting. For me, the big thing about Carver was that life was too short, and that's my problem exactly. I mean, I set out to write novels. Then I decided I didn't have the time to be a novelist and made up my mind to focus on writing short stories instead. By now, I've reached the point where all I can manage is collecting ideas for stories. Looking at Raymond Carver in Safeway—me stopped in my tracks, him with a tub of Haagen-Dazs in his hand—this parallel of time pressures gave me a thousand-volt frisson.

'Belgian chocolate,' Raymond Carver said.

There wasn't anyone else he could have been talking to. I think I tried to smile. Probably, I blushed.

'Oh,' I said, like he had explained some big mystery. 'Right.' I'm a Safeway veteran but I've never developed the knack of small talk with celebrities I admire. I ducked my head and steered my trolley towards the bakery section.

In the early days of bumping into Raymond Carver, I thought my problem was simple: no time to write. 'I have all these ideas,' I told Jill. She was forking cat food out, icing a birthday cake for her friend and pouring a saucepan of boiled parsnips into the colander. 'And no time to do anything with them. Not properly.'

'Reach me that dish,' she said.

'Just this morning I had another one. A great theatrical director-impresario, somebody rich, famous and powerful, the whole shemozzle, somebody who's been on *Desert Island Discs* not once, but twice, somebody who's used to snapping his fingers and bingo-zingo—people jump to it. What would happen if somebody like that really were cast away?'

'I don't know. What?'

'Well, I don't know either. It'd be interesting to find out. But I never will find out, because I haven't got any pigging time, have I?'

'Well, didn't Trollope write all his big fat books before going off to run the Royal Mail every day?'

'Trollope!' The last of the icing farted out of the bag to punctuate my contempt. 'Don't talk to me about Trollope.'

'We're not talking about Trollope. We're talking about you. We always talk about you.'

'Well—that's it with writers. Alan Bennett said so: 'The thing with writers is—'

' "Me, me, me". Tell me about it.'

The Warner Brothers Store in the Arndale was the next place I ran into Raymond Carver. He was watching a Road-runner short on the composite video screens. Nothing ventured, I was thinking when I decided to approach this distinguished writer with a taste similar to my own for escapism shopping.

'How was the Belgian Chocolate?' I asked.

'Oh,' he said. 'You're an ice cream fan, too?'

'Isn't everyone?'

'I guess. I have a problem with compulsive behaviour. Ice cream has helped me a lot.'

'My problem is shortage of time. Too much on my plate.'

'What is it you haven't enough time for?'

'Well.' I sheepished. 'I, I'm a writer.'

'Isn't everyone?' Raymond Carver said.

I thought he was ridiculing me, but then he smiled, and I knew it was only banter, with what I had said about being an ice cream fan.

'I love this guy.' He indicated Wile E. Coyote on the video screens. 'He's such a loser, but he never gives up.'

The *Desert Island Discs* idea didn't go away, but it didn't develop either; there wasn't any time or space in my life to nurse it. Germs of stories would be harassing me as I went to work, taught my adult education class, spent time with Jill, studied for my Open University writing course, attended church, did chores, read, jogged or cooked. I couldn't see much common ground between Raymond Carver and me beyond the pressures of time, but I wanted to see him and talk again. Little did I know how long it would be before that would happen.

There was a week's holiday due, which I had earmarked for developing a piece of work—perhaps the *Desert Island Discs* story. We were walking in the water park, when Jill announced that she wanted us to drive west and spend a long weekend with her parents.

'You go,' I told her. 'You know I'm desperate to get a story finished. I'm desperate to get a story started, for crying out loud.'

'They won't be here forever.'

I trotted out some invective about my need to write and the obstacles there were to that—nothing she hadn't heard before.

'Yes,' she said. 'But why do you need to write?'

Everyone will love me, I thought. I will never be lonely.

When I got down to work on 'Luxury Item', as the *Desert Island Discs* story came to be known, I wasn't happy with the direction the story was taking. The raw material was there all right and there were one or two literary devices I had mustered, but the spark of imagination that had fired the original idea seemed to have dimmed as I handled it. I wished I were ambitious for something more accessible, something with a more defined career path—being a cardiologist, for instance. I was wishing Raymond Carver would show again. I believed that his presence would place some sort of seal on what I was trying to do. I believed Raymond Carver would affirm me.

Sometimes when I was sitting at the keyboard, I would

imagine him sloping about the workroom, lurking big and gentle like some gloomy ministering angel. He would look at the pictures on my wall, the books on my shelves, the stories and plays and novels and poems in the filing cabinet—twenty years of digging down that had led up to this: blocked ideas.

He might examine the music in the workroom. He pulls out a disc and turns it over in his hands. 'You like Mozart?'

'Doesn't everyone?' I say.

Carver smiles and reads the packaging on the disc. He slides it back in place and pulls out another, a Bo Diddley compilation.

'Rock'n'roll—American music is a great passion,' I say. I'm doing all the talking here: silence is hard to handle. 'Everything American has been an obsession.'

'Oh well. I've had my troubles with obsessiveness, too, you know. Did I tell you that already?' Raymond Carver looks my way as he speaks. Then he shrugs—his shoulders rise like two whales in a synchronised swimming event—and he sweeps his Timberlands around the carpet and studies the pictures on my walls. He draws up before the *It's A Wonderful Life* poster.

'Cliché, I know,' I say. 'But it's so powerful. To be shown that you matter, that your life counts.'

Carver shuffles over to the cast iron fireplace, where he pauses by some framed photographs. He lifts a little one and looks at it.

'My Dad,' I tell him. 'He died when I was small.'

Carver looks from the photo to me, then back at the photo.

'Do you think each one of us is George Bailey?' I say. 'Do you think we all need a sort of thumbs-up from some supreme force?'

27

Then Raymond Carver does a funny thing. He opens his tweed jacket with his left hand and, with his right, slides that picture of my Dad into his inside pocket.

I must have looked puzzled.

In Safeway there were always other celebrities I could have engaged in conversation, none of them any substitute for Raymond Carver. Susan Fleetwood, for instance — in town for an Ibsen at the Royal Exchange, which I'd seen.

'Saw your show,' I said.

'And?'

'Good.' In fact, it was a dog. Something of this must have come out in my tone; I could see it in Susan Fleetwood's face. What was the point in being polite about it? 'Maybe a little O.T.T. after he finds out that you've burnt the manuscript.'

'Yes,' she said, and she was happy with this remark, she was vindicated and she was revisiting her frustration. 'I argued that in rehearsal, but in the end I gave in to the director. Ohhh.'

It occurred to me to say more, but the important thing with talking to celebrities in Safeway is to know when to cut loose and make for the checkout.

Time passed. Some things changed and some things didn't. One of the things that changed was life for Jill and me. We had been trying to start a family for about a year and one day it took. We were beside ourselves. By about halfway through the pregnancy, I found all kinds of unexpected thoughts and feelings growing in me. Fathers and children became the dominant theme of my life in those months. I wondered what sort of father I might make. I could hardly remember my own Dad. There were large emotions swelling inside me about this life swelling inside Jill.

'I don't know what a Dad does,' I said to her once.

'Just work out what was missing in your childhood and you'll know what a Dad is supposed to do.'

I did. I thought about that a lot. I read books on parenting, but especially on fathers. And from there I branched out into stuff on children, on love hunger—even on compulsive behaviour, which, I learned, has its roots in the emotional wounds of childhood.

Summer faded out from every leaf in the city. Everything changed colour—every day it seemed. Our life was filled with change; it felt as though the ground was shifting beneath us. Jill was slowing down, settling into what was happening to her body. I gave up teaching that adult education class, I learned to say 'No' to people, I stayed in more. 'Luxury Item', the *Desert Island* short story, sold and on the back of that I had my hopes up high enough to start working on further stories. Everything was changing. There was more time to write and there was, as I said, more time to read. The way I was devouring Father books, it wouldn't be long before I'd be co-hosting a parenting show with Nick Ross.

I would read striking discoveries aloud to Jill: *'A boy's need to be affirmed by his father is as strong as the urge to mate.'*

Yes, there was more time freed up and some of it was for Jill and me.

'It's all about time,' she told me one morning. 'Everything needs time to breathe, to live. Without time and space, everything dies. Extra time has made us happier, hasn't it?'

I remember this conversation well. It was a Saturday and we took the tram into town. In the fresh, golden light, the autumn foliage made the city warm and welcoming. G-MEX reached out and hugged us, the tower of the Refuge Building did a little Fred Astaire soft-shoe shuffle across the rooftops of Oxford Road.

'I like it here,' I said. We had cappuccinos and blueberry muffins in our favourite cafe, mooched in the Pre-Raphaelite room of the City Art Gallery, shopped together and then split up for individual errands. On Market Street, I was so filled with joy and delight that I bought copies of *The Big Issue* from three separate vendors.

I reached M&S for our rendezvous at noon. The place was hiving like a Calcutta bazaar. They were going frantic in Men's Clothing. I had to dance like Lennox Lewis to resist getting swept into Household Furnishing. That was when I looked up and straight into familiar cool, sharp eyes.

'I've been hoping to bump into you again,' I told him. 'I had a sort of daydream about you parading around my workroom.'

His gentle expression was fixed, but he was attending to what I had to say.

'It made me think about what we most want from life. You seemed to be challenging my obsessions.'

The hint of a smile crossed Carver's face. 'Did I?'

This wasn't the way I had foreseen our conversation. There was so much commotion it was hardly possible to stand your ground. Compared to this, Safeway was like a library reading room. I had been bursting with things to say to Raymond Carver, but months had passed and I had changed and now I believed that all my questions amounted to one. It was a question Jill had asked me at the climax of one of our arguments. It was burning my tongue now, but I could only approach asking it in a roundabout way.

'Raymond, why do you write?'

'I told you—I've always had problems with compulsive behaviour.'

Raymond Carver was very vivid there in Marks & Spencer's. His tweed and button-down presence, his brindled hair, his kind face and his large, long frame all felt more delineated than reality. In the distance, I could see Jill approaching. She was scanning the shop floor. She hadn't spotted us.

'I didn't tell you,' I said. 'I'm going to be a Dad.'

'That's fine.'

'I've wanted to talk to you so much. There were so many things. About obsession—you remember we spoke about *It's A Wonderful Life*?'

'We did?'

'Didn't we? I wanted to ask you—'

'I have to go.'

By now, Jill had spotted us and was homing in from the escalators. She was waving a Mothercare carrier bag in the air, oblivious to the writer beside me.

'Here,' he said, reaching inside his jacket. 'This is yours.'

Jill came up and greeted me, looking at Raymond Carver, as I was accepting what he was holding out to me. He gave her a small, gracious nod of his head and walked into the throng, which carried him away. Neither of us moved or spoke until he disappeared from view.

I looked at the photograph of my Dad in my hand.

'What was all that about?' Jill asked.

I put my arms around her. 'Writing,' I said.

After that, the Raymond Carver story arrived at an upbeat coda. For a few sweet weeks the celebrities wouldn't leave me alone. I would be pushing a trolley round Safeway and before I knew it, a household name would be alongside me, in more ways than one. Francois Truffaut, for instance.

'I admire your romanticism so much,' he told me, with emphatic gestures to match.

Again and again it was the celebrities who approached me, not the other way round. And they were always men. Sometimes they wouldn't even speak: Mohammed Ali put an arm over my shoulder, Paul McCartney gave me a thumbs-up in Frozen Vegetables, Samuel Beckett, with a locker-room laugh, clapped me on the back.

The final celebrity blessing wasn't even in a store: one day Bob Dylan rang me at work.

'I just wanted you to know,' he mumbled, 'that you remind me of me.'

I never saw Raymond Carver again.

DID THE STRAND

Bob Lamont sat for longer than he had planned in the concourse at Piccadilly: her train was delayed by almost half an hour. When it finally kissed the buffers, he was one clue short of completing the *Guardian* quick crossword. Strikebreaker, four letters. He knew it; the word was on the tip of his tongue. Something like 'scat' or 'stab', but it just wouldn't come back to him.

The train doors opened and the platform suddenly filled with an ant colony of people. Bob stepped to the left, to the right, and advanced slowly through the crowd, craning his neck to try and see her. He came out of one throng and a space opened up in front of him, only ten metres or so, before the next grouping of passengers. And there she was, coming towards him. A dark brown coat and a voluminous rust scarf. As they converged on each other, he saw that her hair was neat and fresh and her mouth moist and distinct with scarlet lipstick. He could picture her getting out her make-up pouch, opening her compact and painting her lips in the mirror, brushing her hair and maybe her eyebrows were more strongly delineated. It lifted his heart like a dip on a rollercoaster to think of her smartening herself up before they met.

When only a stone's throw separated them, her mouth spread and her eyes crinkled into a heart-warming smile in which love itself seemed to rush to her face. He could feel it practically bursting out of him, too. They came together, clamped arms about one another and kissed, a strong passionate kiss that left Bob light-headed. When they drew apart, it was like divers coming up for air. Without saying anything, she smiled and took his hand and led him back down the platform towards Manchester.

'You're late!' he said.

'Do you good to be kept waiting.' She stopped and turned to him, took his head in her hands and kissed him again. 'Was it awful for you?'

'Agony.' Her drum-shaped green earrings matched her eyes.

On the bus journey to West Didsbury, she told him the latest from Coach Films. They had got her reading scripts and writing reports. 'Somebody must have noticed I have a degree in English,' she said. The scripts were all rubbish, full of stock characters and clichéd plots, like reading parodies, parodies of parodies. Sometimes, though, there were laugh-out-loud moments. Recently, much of the news from Coach Films concerned Marc Berber, the company's managing director. Berber had produced the five films that Coach had completed. More than a year had passed since the last project that went into production and, increasingly, Berber had given up coming into the office. (One theory was that he had become agoraphobic.) The situation caused problems, as no decisions could be made without his approval. Initially, staff would phone him at home, but in the past month, he had stopped answering the phone, so people had begun to seek his approval by telegram.

'Telegram!' Isabelle said with a laugh. 'It does slow things down, but it could get worse. What happens when he stops responding to telegrams? We'll have to get decisions approved by post. Anyway, it's good for me. Colin Roach, Marc Berber's right hand man, likes me. I'm hoping I might be able to manoeuvre my way into some script editing.'

'If you get a script worth editing.'

'Exactly.'

They got off on Palatine Road and walked around the corner to the three-storey redbrick terrace on Goulden Road that housed his flat. Goulden Road used to make him think of the Roxy Music song: 'See La Goulue and Nijinsky do the Strandsky'.

He opened the front door and they climbed the stairs to the first floor where he unlocked the door to his flat. She hung her coat and scarf on a hook in the hall and took him in her arms again and pressed him to her.

'Hello,' she murmured.

He had been to the R&M Deli on Burton Road and bought a selection of things he knew she would like: cabanas, green olives, Polish ham, taramasalata, bagels and pretzels. He chopped tomatoes, cucumber and lettuce for a salad and made dressing with a recipe she had taught him —with oil, vinegar, mustard powder and brown sugar. When it was ready, they sat on the floor in the living room and ate off the coffee table. She had brought him a present, a country LP full of names to enjoy: Skeets McDonald, Bob Wills & His Texas Playboys, The Tennessee Drifters. Country & Western was her new passion and she was trying to get him to share it. He had left a bottle of her favourite wine, Frascati, in the fridge and they drank it now as they listened to Tommy McLain sing 'Sweet Dreams'.

Sometimes, when they were reunited, they took their clothes off as soon as they were indoors and made love and sometimes they ate first. Rarely would they wait until bedtime.

In the early evening, they lay a long time across the bed, talking sleepily and stroking one another's limbs. It was June, a hot day. He got up and went to let in some air. The ropes on the sash window in his bedroom were broken, but if you lifted the window far enough up, the frame jammed in what must have been a warped part of the channels. A soft breeze tickled his skin and he came back and lay down beside her.

Maybe the mood turned before they got to planning the next time they would meet, or maybe that was the moment. He would never know.

'Will you come up in a fortnight?' he asked.

'Up here?' She frowned. 'But it's your turn to come down.'

'I know. It's just that money's short at the moment, and it's so much more expensive to spend the weekend in London than it is here. I'd pay your train fare. To be honest, I'd still be less out of pocket if I paid for your ticket than if I went down.'

'I don't know . . .' Her voice trailed away and he felt that she was waiting for him to give in. Being determined was one of her most apparent traits. He made up his mind to poker-face her out.

'It's difficult,' she finally replied.

'What? Have you got something on that weekend?'

'No. I'm just finding it hard to make a new life when I'm away so much.'

'You're not up here any more than I'm down with you.'

'Yes, but you've been living here a long time. You've already got your circle of friends, haven't you?'

He didn't say anything. He was reluctant to give in, but he was thinking that Humphrey Lennon had a show coming up in Oxford and had offered to pay Bob if he would drive the work down in a rented van. That might help. He was teaching ten hours a week for the WEA and had some rent from a house he owned in Belfast, but he was still some way short of solvent.

'Maybe we should skip a weekend?' she suggested.

He looked at her, alarmed. 'A month is a long time. Wouldn't you mind?'

She was sitting up now and had drawn a sheet over her. 'Of course I'd mind. But we have to be realistic.'

A loud thud startled them. The sound snapped his gaze at once to its cause: the broken sash window had fallen from where it was jammed and slammed down shut. The shock unsettled him.

'You do what you want,' he said, gruffly.

She looked into his face and pulled an expression that said, Don't be like that.

'What?' he said, although he knew what. She kissed him on his cheekbone. 'I wanted this to be a perfect weekend for you,' he said.

'And?' she said, like What's the problem?

For some reason perfection no longer seemed likely, was what he thought, but he knew it would be foolish to say so. Something had shifted in the wind and the idyll of romance they seemed to be walking through as they came down the station platform had been blown away, blown somewhere else—someone else was going to have that weekend.

'I don't know,' he said, although he could see that he knew quite a bit.

She sat up and leaned her back against the wall at the head of the bed. The wallpaper was big, blue flowers on a brown background. The sheet she had pulled over her before fell in folds into her lap and the loveliness of her breasts in this off-kilter moment was a taunt to him.

'The trouble with living apart,' she said, 'is that when you're together it has to perfect.'

He nodded and reached for her hand. She clasped his. 'Let's pretend you just got here,' he told her. 'You came up the stairs, opened the door and didn't stop kissing me until we fell apart, spent.'

She leaned in to kiss his mouth.

'And I sent you to turn over the record and bring me a mug of tea in bed.'

On the bus into the city centre, they still couldn't find their way back to the intimacy and harmony that had been there before they argued.

Bob was taking her to a pub on Thomas Street, close to Tib Street, where tonight there was live music: a Rockabilly band, The Sheiks, he thought she might enjoy. They were good, so he'd heard, and if she liked Country, mightn't she like Rockabilly, too?

They climbed steep stairs to the function room where the gig was to be. The space was only three quarters full, so they were able to get a table with a decent view of the stage. While Bob was at the bar, the MC came on and introduced the support band, two tall blokes with guitars, who were called The Dead Stetsons and turned out to be a country covers act. When they sang 'Funny How Time Slips Away', Isabelle leaned close and shouted in his ear, 'I love this song!' Bob smiled and nodded, pretending to share her enthusiasm. All he knew about Willie Nelson was that he was an old guy with a dodgy haircut.

As their fourth or fifth song began, Bob could see that The Dead Stetsons weren't going to be as winning as their name. One played quite good lead guitar, the other strummed with concrete fingers and they didn't sound like a duo that had spent a lot of time rehearsing. They played another song that Isabelle recognised—'He'll Have

To Go'—but this time she conceded that it wasn't a very good version. Some others in the small crowd thought the same thing.

'Get off, you're crap!' a deep voice boomed.

Bob looked and saw the source: at a table on the other side of the room, a guy with lank hair who wore a shabby, old raincoat. The friend he sat with wore charity shop clothes, too. They didn't look particularly aggressive. To judge by the way they dressed, you would have thought they were unreconstructed Joy Division fans.

'Ohhh,' Isabelle said. 'These two don't deserve that. They're not bad, really.'

Bob took her hand and patted it. Sometimes she was too softhearted.

They sipped their beer and watched glumly as the singers finished their short set. Whatever this final song might have sounded like in its original version, it was a dirge in the hands of The Dead Stetsons. Bob thought it would never end, but when it did, it was with a long, extended note, during which somebody hurled a cigarette packet that struck one of the Stetsons on the cheek. He flinched and broke off from singing. Bob looked over to the hecklers' table and saw a third one who hadn't been there before, a guy in a biker jacket with thick eyebrows and greasy, black hair. He was on his feet and it looked like he was responsible for the projectile. At once, the other singer struck a conclusive chord on his guitar, said 'Thanks,' and the pair of them quickly left the stage.

Isabelle went to the bar, leaving Bob to his thoughts, which kept touching against the impasse over their next weekend. He didn't understand how such a little thing had opened up so much distance between them. He knew he ought to concede and go down to London in a fortnight's time, he knew it was more important to see each other than to be prudent about money, but something was stopping him.

He looked across to where she stood amongst half a dozen people waiting to be served. He knew relationships could end for inconsequential reasons. It had happened to him before, when he told his girlfriend at the time that he was going to Manchester to study. She assumed he was finishing with her, so it had ended even though he was sure that wasn't what either of them had wanted. It made him wary of the inconsequential. He looked at her, trim in her long-sleeved jade T-shirt and denim skirt, and didn't want to imagine what breaking up might be like this time. As he watched her, he saw the man in the biker jacket come up and wait at the bar beside her. He didn't suppose that people who threw things at performers were often going to be sympathetic, but he really didn't like the look of this bloke.

'The barman called me "duck",' Isabelle said, setting his bitter and her white wine down on the table. 'I'm not sure I like being called "duck".'

Bob looked across. The barman resembled Les Dawson. 'I'm sure he meant it kindly.' There was sometimes this precious thing about Isabelle; she often found others wanting. Oh these people! she would say.

'It's not exactly a compliment. Does it mean that I waddle?'

'It means that he was being friendly to you. That's all.'

The Sheiks were lively. The guitarist had a warm, fat sound and the upright bass-player underscored everything with a throbbing beat. The singer was a large guy with a quiff and Morrissey glasses. He loomed over a fold-back speaker, leaning his torso and the mic stand out towards the audience. His belly swelled his shirt at the waist and he gestured a lot with his right hand. He wore an incongruous grey suit. The only song Bob recognised was Gene Vincent's 'Rocky Road Blues', but he was enjoying the set and he could see that Isabelle was having a good time, too.

Thomas Street, when they emerged into it, was deserted. Some of the streetlights weren't working, so they moved quickly, eager to reach somewhere better lit, more populated. They headed east and then south towards Piccadilly Gardens, where they would get their bus. They were in a narrow, dark street when they heard singing behind them. Bob turned and saw that it was the hecklers from the gig, the three that had given The Dead Stetsons a hard time. The song they were singing contained a lot of crude references. They were an ugly bunch. They were drunk and they gave off a bad vibe. He took Isabelle's hand and increased his pace.

'Honey, honey!' one of them, rather bizarrely, shouted.

Bob hoped this wasn't being addressed at them, but they were the only other people on this side street. He turned to look at Isabelle and found her looking at him. Just at that moment, one of the three men made a hooting sound, an animal noise. The meaning was unclear, but it didn't sound friendly.

'What about a smile, love?' one of them called—the one in the raincoat, Bob thought; it sounded like the voice that had heckled The Dead Stetsons.

'Don't make eye contact,' Isabelle told him.

He knew that, though. He knew he wasn't going to make eye contact and he knew that they had to get through to Piccadilly as fast as they could, reach a place where there were lights and other people.

'Nice legs!' another one brayed.

'Thanks,' Bob shouted over his shoulder. He thought humour might deflate the tension. It didn't.

The kafuffle of running feet came next and Bob felt the first wash of adrenaline in his belly as the three on the opposite pavement overtook them and crossed the road diagonally, cutting him and Isabelle off.

The guy in the biker jacket was tall and broad-shouldered. He looked strong and aggressive. The one in the raincoat was reasonably big, too. Only the third man was smaller than Bob. Dark stubble covered his jaw and his forehead sloped back sharply from his brow.

They came to a halt in front of Bob and Isabelle, but after his Doc Martin boots had stopped, the one in the raincoat's body appeared to carry on with the momentum. He almost toppled over.

All three of them seemed brutish to Bob. You could find people like them in any pub in the land, but you didn't want them blocking your path. Piccadilly, he knew, was only a stone's throw away and although there would be scores of people there, scores of people almost within earshot, the spot where he and Isabelle stood seemed very isolated.

The last time he was in a fight, Bob was eleven years old and he lost. He wasn't comfortable in arguments, let alone fights, and a tangle with these three would be a massacre.

The men were a dozen feet in front. Bob and Isabelle were still walking towards them. The jeans of the one in the biker jacket were smudged with dark stains, like oil. Perhaps he really was a biker. He pictured this man producing a bike chain and wielding it at them, swinging it in the air, as people in situations like this did in the movies. This was exactly like a situation in the movies. It was certainly nothing like life, not his life.

'Come on,' he mumbled and led her to the other side of the road.

'That's not friendly,' the stubbly one said. 'That's not nice.'

They were a little closer to Piccadilly now; maybe if they ran, they could reach it ahead of their pursuers. But that would be undignified. Besides, Isabelle was wearing heels.

'What you doing walking your woman out round dark streets at this time of night?' the one in the raincoat said.

'That's not taking very good care of her,' the stubbly one said.

The three were walking up the middle of the street now. As far as Bob could tell, the biker had yet to speak, which added to his menace.

'How about lending us some dosh?' the one in the raincoat said.

'I don't know you,' Bob said.

'You'd like to do your bit to help out, though, wouldn't yuh?'

Bob stopped. 'Look, we're just minding our own business here. We've been out to see a band and now we're going home. Okay?' He could feel a tremor in his legs. He tried his best to stop it showing.

'Yeah,' the one in the raincoat said. 'It's late. We should be getting home ourselves. C'mon, lads, eh?'

'Oh aye!' the stubbly one went.

Up until this point, Bob could see them out of the corner of his eye, but now they stepped onto the pavement and followed directly behind him and Isabelle. Not to be able to see them was more unsettling. In his chest, his heart was hammering.

'How much you got?' the one in the raincoat growled.

'Ignore them,' Isabelle said.

They were very close to Piccadilly; they had rounded a bend in the street and could see lights and cars up ahead. They both increased their pace at the same time.

'Is that what you think we want?' the same voice said. D'you think we want your money?'

Bob could see the implied threat here—that Isabelle, not money, was what they wanted. Ahead, where the street abutted Piccadilly Gardens, he could see people walking by. Surely they were near enough now to run. This close to civilisation, surely the game was up? Surely that was all these three wanted, a game, some sport at the expense of harmless passers-by like him and Isabelle?

He heard somebody move, footfalls coming faster as they overtook and drew up a few feet ahead. The man in the raincoat now stood halfway between Bob and Isabelle and Piccadilly Gardens. The other two were still behind them. He took Isabelle's arm and kept walking. If the men attacked at this stage, wouldn't somebody intervene? Fear was making Bob feel sick.

'I bet she's a good fuck,' the one in the raincoat said.

With that, Isabelle erupted, hurtling towards Raincoat, thumping into his ribcage with her right shoulder and knocking him off his feet. Bob thought that in her anger she had taken leave of her senses. She had made a bad situation a whole lot worse. There was nothing else to do, though, but run, too. Slowed by drink, the stubbly one and the biker started after them a few seconds later than they might have, bawling incoherently.

As he sprinted behind her, Bob saw beyond Isabelle what she herself must have seen before she made her move: a black cab depositing its fare on the north side of Piccadilly Gardens. In seconds, Isabelle had swept past the couple on the pavement getting change from the cabbie and crashed through the open back door onto the bench seat. Bob tumbled in after her and slammed the door shut. He heard a sound like a bolt shooting and guessed that the cabbie must have pressed a button to lock the doors. He saw the alarmed faces of the passengers who had just got out of the cab and then the driver turned, resting his elbow on the seatback and said, 'In bother?'

'They were trying to mug us,' Isabelle said.

'Aye well,' the driver said. He slipped the cab in gear and puttered forward. While the vehicle was moving off, unbearably slowly, the biker slapped into its side, and hammered the roof with his fist. As the cab pulled away, he spat and a slobber of spit landed on the window through which Bob and Isabelle were looking.

'Nice,' the cabbie said.

At home, although Bob tackled in two or three ways the subject of what had just happened, Isabelle seemed not to want to discuss it and for the rest of the weekend, made no mention of it. Then, and on the phone later, he offered to come down the next but one Friday.

'You're right,' she told him on the phone. 'It's silly to get yourself into debt.'

Whenever he thought of it, the knowledge that he had failed her in an important way that weekend preyed on his mind. Long afterwards, he would yearn for Isabelle's naked legs on his bed that evening at Goulden Road, though the moment was gone, so far over the horizon he would never be able to summon it back. But he would remember Goulden Road and wonder if, when you died, you could fly over your life and revisit the times you longed to retrieve, and relive them as often as you wanted, much as you would at exhibitions, returning to the start to walk round your favourite canvases again. He would remember Isabelle's legs on that bed in Goulden Road and whisper, 'See La Goulue and Nijinsky—did the strand.'

CARCASSES

IT'S FREE FOR PENSIONERS at our local pool on Tuesdays and Thursdays. I never used to, but since my husband died, week in, week out, I swim. I hate having to look at all the undressed carcasses, mine included, but I enjoy the exercise and I'm not the only one.

Here we are. There must be fifteen of us on a good day and I know all of them at least by name. Most of us went to the Public Elementary School together. The streets outside, where we've lived our lives, are miserable-looking, Edwardian red-bricks, and it's peculiar to me that our lifetimes have been passed out there and now we're reaching the end here in the bright, glinting pool, built only five years ago—the day before yesterday, really.

Picture us, wearing our decaying flesh, crossing and recrossing the pool like sluggardly dredgers passing across a bay.

I'm early today, but I might just as well be late. I don't have any regard for time—I gave it up. There's a clock on the front-room mantelpiece, but that's all. I don't wear a watch.

The blackboard beneath the pool clock says 83°F in shaky chalk, but it never is. They always say it's that and it's always colder than they say, because 83°F would be warm, wouldn't it?

I'm at the yellow steps, which take you very gradually up to your waist in chilly, sharp blue, but I stop there and look around. There's Mr & Mrs Johnny Weissmuller, as I call them—the diving stars. Neither one of them is any

younger than me, but she practises and he analyses her diving like she was in training for an event. When she
completes a dive, never well, he's waiting for her at the side
and she'll give him all her attention as he bends from the
waist, brings his arms together above his head and gives it
some post-match analysis. I wouldn't know whether he's a
good diver or not—I've never seen him dive. But he looks
the part all right: high shoulders, broad ribcage, flat belly.
What in the name of goodness is he doing with a flat belly
at his age? Johnny and his missus are like a pair of
teenagers who've just started going with each other. I don't
know how she's put up with a lifetime of that.

Johnny nods at me, very formal. Of course, I stretch a big
smile back at him.

Nan Faulkner is in, wading around the shallow end. Her
costume's only wet to the waist and there's an empty hol-
low in it up above, where her right breast should be. I
thought they gave you pads to stick in there. I mean, the
rest of us have feelings, don't we? I don't think Nan's all
there anyway.

I swim a width and turn onto my back to wet my hair. I
used to wear a white rubber cap, but I stopped. You would-
n't believe how often I've had people asking about it.
Wasn't I wearing a cap anymore? Wasn't I bothered about
getting my hair wet? Wouldn't my head be cold without it?

'Look around,' I'd tell them. 'Are any of this lot dying of
pneumonia?' Worst of them all was Esta McKeever. She
went on and on and I held my tongue as long as I could, seeing as her husband had died not long since. I knew how she
was feeling: I'd been through it myself. What with one
thing and another, she'd had a bad twelve months: they'd
amputated his right leg at the knee—cancer—in March
and by August he was dead.

I turn and begin a length, which brings me along by Gordon, the attendant. He sits in his high chair, staring without focus. He looks like a tennis umpire waiting for a match that's never going to happen.

I worry for him. He never acknowledges your presence. In fact, we didn't even know his name until Esta McKeever became a Born Again and found it out. She'd never spoken to him before. None of us had. Gordon's very interested in the young girls, especially when they're walking about or waist-high in the water. As far as you can tell, he's not interested in anything else. Today, as he very often is, Gordon is wearing a Coq Sportif T-shirt. Very fitting.

I see Jean Adair is sat at the other end, her arms spread out in a crucifix on the poolside, so I make a swift turnaround.

'Hullo there,' is all I say to Jean, but I can't help seeing the dimpled, slack skin hanging off her arms. Given an inch, she can whine on for as long as anyone will let her, moaning away about whatever debris floats to the surface of her mind: her husband, vandals, semi-skimmed milk, her new diet or the Free State. I can't listen to it anymore, especially not the diet bit. The world has diets on the brain. I mean, where would the newspapers be without diets and the Royal Family? It makes me sick.

A girl, maybe twenty, shimmies in from the changing rooms. She doesn't even flinch as she passes the draughts from the emergency doors, although that doesn't irritate me as much as her hair. My heart sinks, it's so healthy and strong. I've seen wigs with healthier-looking hair than I've got. I blame the perming solution. I mean, it smells bad enough.

I'm so busy being eaten up by this hair that I don't see Esta McKeever until I'm on top of her.

'Your sonar's not functioning, Helen.'

'Oh! Sorry, love,' I say.

I think a lot about Esta since she became a Born Again. Previous to that, I didn't have strong feelings about her either way. She was never short of a man when she was a wee lassie and there were those who held that against her. But to me Esta's always been all right. I just never used to think about her like I have since she got God.

I suppose I'd like to believe. I'd like to believe in Santa Claus, too, but I can't anymore. It's hard to remember that far back, but I've a feeling I probably believed in God when I did believe in Santa Claus. It was a long time ago anyway, I know that much.

'Are you stopping or swimming the Irish Sea today?' Esta asks.

I give a short laugh and settle with my back to the wall. From my new position, I see Mrs Weissmuller dive from the far side, her cellulite wobbling as she springs off the edge. She enters the water with all the grace of a pantomime cow.

'You're looking well,' Esta says.

'I am not. I look like a transvestite. Shame on you: "Thou shalt not lie".'

'"Build each other up".'

'Eh?'

'What Paul said.'

'Paul who?'

'"Paul who" yourself. Paul who wrote half the New Testament. That Paul. We're having a special charity dinner at church on Sunday. You wouldn't like to come, would you?'

'You're dead right. I would not.'

'The idea is third world food at first world prices and all the money goes to the hungry in Africa.'

'Did it ever cross your mind that if God wanted people in Africa to eat better, He'd send them a McDonalds?'

Esta looks at me with patient good humour. She's used to me. 'There's enough food in the world for everyone, Helen, but God leaves us to sort it out. Free will, you see.'

'So God depends on the likes of you to do His work for Him? Ach. You'd think He could do better.'

'Oh no. It's not a question of ability. It's availability that counts.'

'You're like a parrot, you.' It really gets on my wick the way she spills out these polished phrases she's picked up at that church. 'There's no way I could go to your church. I'd need subtitles to understand what they were saying.'

Esta laughs and tells me she supposes I'm right. Quite disarming—it's a wee knack she has. Jean Adair floats up to us. She's a sight, so she is, with her red goggles and green and orange cap, not to mention those varicose veins.

'Awful cold, isn't it?' she says, and I can see that we're trapped here at the deep end.

'I'm sorry about Rover,' Esta says.

'Aye, it's all very sad.'

'What about Rover?' I ask.

Esta is shaking her head at me.

'Put down,' says Jean. 'He was hit by the lemonade lorry, a week past on Thursday. Honest though, it was all for the best. He was better off out of it.'

'You'll miss him,' Esta says.

'Oh, I will.' A few lengths later, Esta floats up to me on her back. She doesn't do the backstroke, exactly. She just kicks herself along, lying there with her face to the ceiling, no arms. Like the Venus de Milo.

There's a silence. We both sit with our backs to the wall in the shallow end. I nod at Johnny Weissmuller and his

51

missus. 'She's like a sea elephant,' I say but Esta says nothing back. I've noticed this about her—doesn't like to gossip anymore. 'Oh come on. It's not exactly character assassination.'

' "The wicked will not inherit the Kingdom of God," Paul says in his letter to the Corinthians. "Neither idolaters, nor thieves, nor slander—" '

I'm sorely tempted to say, You shouldn't be reading other people's mail. But in fact I tell her, 'Spare me. You Bible-bashers are all the same. You think you're the only ones that know a flippin' thing about right and wrong. Do you think God's got so little to do that he'd care what I say about the Weissmullers' diving club?'

'Since you mention it, I think He's bothered about everything.'

'Oh well,' I say. 'I wouldn't know as much about Him as you, Esta.'

'You could if you wanted to.'

'Well, I don't want to.' Honestly. How do these things get started? It just happens.

'I'm sorry you feel that way,' Esta says.

And she is—you can tell. ' Don't be.' And I swim off. I could have seen her far enough.

As I slowly make my way towards the deep end, I'm feeling more upset than I ought to be. I'm going over and over how God is all right for those that can believe in Him. For the rest of us, He's like a luxury item: it looks nice in the shop window, but you know you'll never be able to have it for yourself. And I'm angry with Esta for being pleasant when I'm pushing her not to be and for wanting to do what's right. I'm still thinking about this when I turn for another length and see Johnny Weissmuller dive off the side and plunge perfectly into the water. He surfaces and powers towards the middle of the pool. Here, Esta is doing her Venus de Milo impression. Johnny reaches her in a few fluid strokes. I'm wondering what's going on. He stops and stands by her in the water. I keep swimming towards them.

'Oh no!' Johnny shouts in his mahogany voice.

At this, Gordon the attendant jumps off his high chair, takes two dancer's steps and dives in, fully clothed. I've never seen him do anything in a hurry before. It's magnetic.

When I reach Esta, Gordon has just pulled up beside her and lowered his feet to the pool floor.

'There's nothing you can do,' Johnny tells him. 'There's nothing anyone can do.'

'What?' I say. I can see Esta, laid out on the water, her eyes stopped still, fixed on the ceiling. I can see a pink flush in them, lots of little pink capillaries. You can't be dead and have bloodshot eyes, can you?

'But she was just—' I say.

'I know,' Johnny says. 'I know.'

I'm thinking he has watched too many people dying in films for his own good. I'm thinking that it's maybe my fault, that I upset her to death. I'm as surprised as he is to find myself whimpering in Johnny Weissmuller's arms.

Later, in the showers, I'm stood in the too-hot torrent which drills into my shoulders. There's a full quota of carcasses in there: me and three others, each one standing like a waxwork, silent, dripping soft, stretched flesh.

In my mind, I see her floating and wonder how many yards she drifted after she'd gone, how long it was before Johnny made his epic dive. I wonder if Esta's soul just left the swimming pool and went straight to God, or was she disappointed at the end? And I carry on wondering about it.

53

THE URBAN SPACEMEN

EVEN THOUGH HE hadn't expressed any interest in close encounters when I first knew him, Bill Kinnaird was a man with a lot going for him. In those days, he owned an Italian sports car finished in racing red, quite a beauty.

'Revs like a dentist's drill; handles like a pre-historic bird,' is what he used to say.

There was also the awe-inspiring record collection, which included Little Richard deletions, not to mention Charlie Parker 78s. Plus Bill's faultless grasp on the ephemera of popular culture. I mean, how often do you meet somebody whose conversation ranges from General Jumbo's radio-controlled model army to the cast lists of *Randall & Hopkirk, (Deceased)*? But, as I say, no talk of close encounters at that stage.

I think Bill's problems began in the summer of 1983, when his wife left him—and came back. During Elaine's absence, Bill consoled himself by painting a life-size Elvis Presley—fat, Las Vegas-era Elvis—on the living-room wall. Also, there was his new friend, Kath. He said she reminded him of Julie Christie in *Billy Liar*. Apparently she left the aroma of coconuts in her slipstream. Then Elaine wanted to come back. Bill's one condition was that the Elvis on the wall had to stay. No more coconuts, though.

If Bill's difficulties began with Elaine's return, the decline of socialism was the clincher. The 80s and 90s hadn't been the easiest time to be a socialist. Bill was very active in our local Labour Party, which had always taken some degree of optimism in itself, but as the Thatcher gov-

54

ernment racked up one term of office after another, hope died in him. It must have been somewhere around here that Bill discovered *Close Encounters Of The Third Kind*. He took to it like a duck to orange sauce. You don't have to be Sigmund Freud to guess that he identified with Richard Dreyfuss looking for redemption in the sky. He was very excited. It became an obsession. Films about contact with aliens kept Bill going through the rest of the 80s and into the 90s, when things went from bad to worse. He saw the TV coverage of the general election defeats through those years. Then his Italian sports car was traded in for a Scandinavian hatchback—a beige Scandinavian hatchback.

'All right, all right,' he protested. 'But no way am I voting SDP.'

And then—children arrived.

To celebrate the birth of the first one, a few of us met at The Elevation, a pub we liked over by the university. Bill spent the night sipping brandies and handing out those square-packed Swiss cigars.

'Joseph Kinnaird,' he gushed.

'Joseph K.,' I went. 'Straight out of Kafka.'

'You can see him in Primary School, can't you?' Bill said. '"Joseph? The Headmaster wants to see you. Don't ask why".'

Everybody laughed. We didn't realise then the grave effect kids were going to have on the things that made Bill Bill. Babies two and three eventually meant that his glorious record collection was banished to the roof space. Can you imagine the ignominy of having to lug a couple of dozen favourites down a Slingsby ladder every month?

The final blow was a double-whammy which began with the '92 election defeat—crushing in itself, Labour had come so close—and ended less than a week later. We were in The Elevation. Quite innocently, I asked Bill if he had managed to get his Volvo welded. He shook his head. He looked like Walter Matthau at a funeral. 'Gloomy' is not the word.

'Gone,' he said.

I asked him what he was doing for a car.

'What am I doing for a car?' he cried. 'What am I doing for a car? I'm driving a Luton-built box, Alistair. That's what I'm doing for a car.'

I groaned sympathetically. I had to rub my face with my hand. I was perplexed, that's all I can say.

'So, if anyone mentions transport,' he warned, 'I arrived here by matter transference. All right?'

I'm not sure how long afterwards it was that we made our big decision. We were in the front room at Bill's house. The carpet was littered with gaudy plastic toys. Under the telly was a stack of sell-through videos with distressing titles: *Bedknobs And Broomsticks, An American Tail*—that sort of thing. Worst of all, though, was the tape with 'My Favourite Martian' in Bill's handwriting on the spine and, written over that in a childish scrawl, 'Postman Pat'. Kind of horrifying.

'Why do men play bowls?' Bill asked me.

'Sorry?' I said.

Bill repeated the question.

I said I didn't know.

'Well,' he replied. 'It isn't to get fit, we know that.'

I could understand what he was saying. I'd seen those old men playing in Chorlton Park. You threw a bowl up to one end of the green, and then you threw it back down again. There didn't seem a lot of point in that. What had struck me most about bowls was the way all the bowlers were called Eric, Walter or Albert. Funny.

'No,' Bill continued. 'The reason men play bowls is the same reason Richard Dreyfuss went off chasing alien mother-ships: to get out of the house, right. The reason men play bowls is to get away from their women and talk about the things in life that really matter. Like who produced 'I'm The Urban Spaceman' by The Bonzo Doo Dah Band or which episodes of *Get Smart* Mel Brooks wrote. You see?'

I saw.

There's more—but not much—to bowls than meets the eye. In England in the 16th century, the Puritans banned the game because it was too much fun. At that time they had bowling hooligans the way they have soccer hooligans now. You can get a hint of what those 16th century bowling thugs must have been like when you stand by the green in Chorlton Park and listen as heckling rises above the rush of wind through the beech trees.

'Half a yard, Walter, half a yard!' they go and:

'Good wood, Albert.'

Maybe there are so many fossils on a bowling green because playing bowls makes you live longer.

John was the only other bowler who was about our age; nobody else came within a decade of it. I remember the day we met John. It was our second or third evening at bowls. I remember it because I was getting something off my chest. I was confessing to Bill that I thought I might be starting to like Bruce Springsteen.

'Get a grip,' Bill told me. 'Bloody Nora. Bruce is rock's Arnold Schwarzenegger.'

I bent and tossed down the manicured turf. My jack

over-carried into the ditch.

'Yeah,' I told Bill, 'but you have to admit he can write lyrics. He's good on coming to terms with aging. Look at 'Hungry Heart'. That song says a lot about my life.'

'You haven't got a hungry heart,' Bill said. 'Your heart has bulimia.'

John appeared then. One of us must have flung a bowl down towards the jack, because John's opening words have stayed with me.

'You know,' he said, 'I believe you would improve your game very considerably if you followed through with your bowling arm.'

I turned around to see this gawky bloke in navy blue. He had an asinine smile.

'Very considerably,' he repeated. His voice was adenoidal and grated like sandpaper, but there was no accent to betray his origins. He could have been from anywhere between Calgary and Canberra. He introduced himself, setting one of his suede Hush Puppies forward on the turf and extending his hand to each of us in turn.

'Manchester lads born and bred?' he said. 'Sons of the cotton, eh? Decided to take up bowls?'

'Yes,' Bill said. 'Forced into it, really.'

'Tell him about your car,' I suggested, but Bill shot a look at me that shut me right up.

John said the gentle pace of the game had drawn him.

'Tremendously relaxing!' he exclaimed. 'There's nothing like it where I come from.'

Of course, we wanted to know where John came from.

'A long, long way away,' was what he told us.

The next thing that happened to Bill was Majorca. Elaine decided she wanted the family to go for a beach holiday and Majorca was the place she had in mind.

'Majorca,' Bill said one evening, as my carefully considered bowl barrelled into the ditch. 'I'm a boy who likes an art gallery or two. What am I going to do on a beach in Majorca for a fortnight? Tell me that.'

I looked up and mustered what I hoped was an expression of dismay. Bill stared off into the trees for a moment. 'You know,' he said. 'I wish I had a strange urge to build a mountain on the dining-room table.'

The look on his face, the tone of his voice—it was quite affecting.

Suddenly, John was standing next to us; he had a habit of appearing at your elbow that way.

'Hello, chaps!' he said. 'How are you keeping?'

Bill told him how he was keeping.

'Not to worry,' John said. 'I have every confidence that things will improve. Recovery is just around the corner.'

John had an unusual way of expressing himself.

I didn't hear about it until the next day, but during that conversation Bill noticed a green glow coming out of John's bowling case. When he told me, neither of us passed comment—although later in the week Bill said he was worried about that green glow.

Soon we were playing bowls every night. We wanted to know more about John. Next time he showed up in the park, we put him on the spot; Bill asked him what he did for a living. John said he worked at the University. Economics. Bill pressed him. John said his job was to warn people about the consequences of continuing in the way they were going.

'Oh. I get it,' Bill said, although Yours Truly didn't.

We retired to The Elevation. Bill asked me if I had ever

59

seen *The Day The Earth Stood Still*, which of course I had. He knew I had.

'Then what,' Bill wanted to know, 'was Michael Rennie's purpose in coming to Earth?'

'To stop war.'

'Yep,' Bill said. 'But to be precise, he came to warn mankind about the consequences of continuing in the way it was going.'

Earnest discussion followed—we even met for lunch the following day. The point at issue was simple: had John parked his saucer behind the bushes in Chorlton Park, or was Bill guilty of building a mountain on the dining-room table?

We didn't dwell on the second possibility.

'Let's say he is,' Bill said. His mind was clicking, flicking like a pinball machine. 'Why? What's his mission? In *The Man Who Fell To Earth*, David Bowie came for minerals to save his dying civilisation. Not so threatening. In *This Island Earth*, the visitors were engaged in a kind of interplanetary brain-drain. Less benign, but harmless when compared to *Invasion Of The Bodysnatchers*, where the aliens took over human bodies—'

I had to interrupt him: 'So what has John come for? To do an extensive study of obscure Earth games?'

We only saw John one more time. Naturally, we were in Chorlton Park. I asked Bill what was happening about Majorca.

'Aw, don't mention it,' he replied. He played a shot that went wide of the jack. 'Should have stuck with the socialism, you know. More my line than bowls.'

'Ah!' a familiar, nasal voice cried out. 'That word—"socialism". Considerable mention is made of this in your national newspapers, and yet nobody here talks about it. I am interested, I must confess.'

Which is how Bill came to be explaining socialism, collective responsibility and the history of the Labour movement in Great Britain to John, open brackets, no known surname, close brackets, Potential Alien.

'Where I come from,' John said at one point, 'there is certainly nothing like this.'

We never saw him again, although we often talked about him.

In The Elevation one night shortly afterwards, Bill described a dream he had had. The dream was very real to him and he made it very vivid for me.

Bill and Elaine and the children were on a sun-soaked beach. Maybe this was Majorca, maybe a Greek island. Everybody he knew was on the beach with him, everybody he knew in fact and everybody he knew vicariously. His relatives and his friends, splashing in the waves, playing ball-games on the sand—although the balls they were kicking, throwing or rolling were planets and stars. These heavenly bodies were silver, the way we see them from the surface of Earth, but also red, yellow and orange, blue and brown, as they might appear close to. The movements of all these balls in their various games—soccer, volleyball, cricket, rounders, bowls—formed a swirling, sweeping mechanism.

As well as Bill's friends and family, all the important people in his life were present, people he knew only from a distance. Little Richard was opening his piano lid, his suit as twinkling and silver as the spheres that spanned the blue sky above the shore. When the lid was fully opened, green light seeped out and bathed Richard's skin emerald. Elvis stood a little way off, lithe and stark-white in a karate suit, waving his arms around and around in smooth martial arts movements that mirrored the clockwork motion of all the balls in all the ball-games.

A perfect 50s B-movie flying saucer sat, black and white, on the sand. Its door opened, and David Bowie and Richard Dreyfuss emerged alongside a giant robot. The robot was sheathed in smooth armour and it waved in slo-mo to nobody in particular, not the Queen's metronome wave, but a circling one, like a window cleaner working his chamois.

Everyone on the beach approached the saucer, drawn to the giant robot. Elaine held their youngest up for a better view and stood next to the two of them was Roger Moore in his safari suit. Bill was on the other side of Elaine, a child clamped to either shoulder.

The robot reached into his flying saucer and began to throw discs in the air: His Master's Voice 78s and CBS Long Players, Parlophone 45s, glittering compact discs — all of them spinning and turning but never falling.

The people gathered there watched, but nobody reached up to try and catch any of the objects moving back and forth above their heads. The robot stretched a hand into the saucer again and flung more objects out to join the kaleidoscope in the air: paperbacks and videotapes, blue plastic letter Ks, scale-model Ferraris and a radio-control handset, it's aerial pointing, swinging, drawing circles — a conductor's baton directing the dance of all the shapes that the robot cast into the air.

And as the galaxies of spheres and oblongs and letters traced their paths above everybody on the beach, the robot began to take off its sheer, grey armour, under which was Julie Christie.

Then there was a shift in the dream and the saucer was rising slowly, slowly over the beach and Julie Christie was looking through an oval window at Bill.

'She had that expression of bittersweet regret,' he told me. 'You know the one. And she was mouthing something to me as the saucer tilted and dipped to maybe twenty feet from me. Her lips formed the words in a sudden extreme close-up. Then the saucer hit like warp-factor ten—disappeared into the wide, blue yonder. And though I couldn't hear what Julie Christie was saying, the next moment I knew, because I was hugging Elaine and the kids and Elaine was looking into me, her blue eyes wide and open, and saying, "I'm in love with you again". And I knew that was what Julie Christie had been saying, too: "I'm in love with you again".'

THE LIFE CLASS

NOBODY KNEW WHAT we got up to in the life class. We didn't fully realise ourselves; what we did crept up on us slowly, cleverly. This was years ago. These days I've stopped drawing altogether. Sometimes I wish I hadn't, but it's clear to me now that the life class was something I did, not for the drawing, but because I had to find a path out of my life. I had to find a path out and follow it.

I was so eaten into then. My soul must have looked like a piece of Jarlsberg. A friend of mine once told me she had had a lover who beat her. I found that hard to take in at the time, but now I wonder if the way my husband treated me was any better.

My life wasn't my own. My sons were day-pupils at a public school. They played rugby or cricket, depending on the season, three times a week. They wore clean, white shirts each day. I'm sure you can imagine, the washing and ironing I did, with these and my husband's shirts, was incredible. It felt like a punishment.

I was young—I married much too young—and there was no one I could confide in. Before the marriage, my closest friend had been my sister Audrey, but immediately after the wedding, my husband took me to Cumbria, where a new job awaited him. His sins—sins of omission, to begin with—mounted day by day. He never lifted a finger to help me, and, on top of the laundry, ours was a large house, which required a good deal of attention. He would remember my birthday and promise me a present later. It would never come. He lectured me on my cooking, he who never boiled an egg, and he would have liked to tell me what to wear. I was less than a person to him, when I should have been more than any other on earth.

We had been thirteen years married when he told me he was having an affair with May Caldwell, the wife of his oldest and best friend. I don't think he told me to absolve his guilt: Matthew was born with the conviction, very convenient, that he is always right. The reason he told me, I suspect, was simply to discuss it with a third party. Since his best friend was unavailable for comment on his wife's affair, I was the only alternative. It wasn't a discussion so much, anyway. I lay there in our bed, bruised like a pomegranate, and leaked slow tears onto my pillow. He talked to himself.

There were other slights, different pressures which I leave out here, but in general this was the background to my joining the life class. The wonder is that it took me so long to do something about finding a release. I saw the adult education classes advertised in our local paper. I had had a flair for drawing at school and was taken with the idea of going to a life class. It took me a few days to make a decision—I was such a shrinking violet in those days.

I remember at the first class wondering whether I should be able to stick it or not. Most of the students were pensioners, and there was something rather doddery, rickety, about the group. As well, the class seemed so well-knit— they all appeared to be friends—that I thought I would never fit in. It was the man who took the class who caused this feeling to pass.

Our teacher, you see, was a professional buffoon. (His parents must have been in on the joke from the beginning, for they had christened him John Constable.) He told us what Lowry or Van Gogh, Matisse or Picasso would do in certain circumstances, told us which exhibitions included his own work, but most of all meandered through the room sprinkling light, punning jokes.

'Ak-chulleh,' he would say, 'I had my first exhibition there when I was one year old. My mother took me along to see some show and had to change my nappy. So I had my first exhibition when I was only one. It's all true.'

He would often tell the same story twice, even three times, but he wasn't a bad sort, and occasionally he would teach us something of use.

I hadn't imagined I would be embarrassed by naked flesh, and I wasn't. I suppose I had conjectured about some sexual thrill when a man came to model for us — I presumed there would be men as well as women. There wasn't any titillation, though. I found I was always absorbed in trying to reproduce the figure before me; it didn't make much difference what sex it was. In this absorption, for two hours every week I was able to forget about everything. After a couple of months, I was even able to see an improvement in my technical ability. It was very satisfying.

For a year, there was my developing technique and old Constable shuffling about, telling his daft yarns, and a succession of models — six in all, I think. Mostly, they were women. These same six people came to us, in turn, for three weeks at a time, so that, by the third session, I for one was heartily sick of looking at the same body. They were all young, by which I suppose I mean under thirty, and all physically less than perfect: too fat, too thin, plain, ugly.

I would sit before them, a mere ten feet distant, and wonder a little at their stillness, but even more at what brought them to do this. True, it was better paid by the hour than shop work, but how many hours would they be able to get in a week? In a small town like ours, not many. I puzzled over what would be going through their heads as they sat stock still. Would they have erotic fantasies? Sitting nude in public, being ogled by a dozen people, I believed I would. I wondered if our male models perhaps thought of me (surely the other women were all too old to be objects of desire?). I knew some of our old men had sex in mind: once, when Constable placed a pert girl with her back to us, Mr. Faulkner, a mole of a man, moved during the break to a position where he could savour her fully frontal.

The first sign of any strangeness at the life class occurred one day in spring when a rather more mature model turned up. I would say she was about sixty and none of us had seen her before.

'I'm new, ' she said. 'Where do I go?'

We pointed her to the cubicle beneath the stencilled sign:

THIS CHANGING ROOM IS EXCLUSIVELY FOR THE
USE OF MODELS

THE PRINCIPAL

No doubt her appearance naked, moments later, was a disappointment to Mr Faulkner. She took a seat on the dais and adopted a comfortable position. Her arms were thick with loose flesh, her breasts sat sloppily over two, three or four flaccid folds of skin on the belly beneath. Her face was dry and puffy and the backs of her hands dappled with age.

Holding our pencils loosely, as we had been taught, we began to rough her outline. That was when it happened — the thin end of the wedge, if you like. Mrs Munroe was the last person any of us would have expected it from, though nobody could have expected it at all. She was a daunting, slightly aristocratic woman with a very clipped pre-war accent. She had not even the hint of a sense of humour. I secretly disliked her for her aplomb.

Not everybody noticed it, but I saw her go into the cubicle that was "exclusively for the use of models". She swept the curtain to noisily enough, but most of the people in that room were at least partially deaf. Of course, I wondered what she was up to.

When she emerged, Mrs. Munroe was—I should have guessed it—naked as a newborn baby. Her skin swayed about her like an outsized suit as she took a seat beside the model. She still wore her pink, winged glasses, which added a touch of the ridiculous to what was already bizarre enough.

'You don't mind, do you, Mr Constable?' Mrs. Munroe said, as if she had taken some of his sugar without asking. 'I simply thought that if this lady can do it, then anyone can.'

Laughter and impromptu applause broke out amongst the other students. One of them flared his eyes incredulously at me. 'No, no,' Constable replied, laughing somewhat himself. 'Ak-chulleh, we can have two models then.'

'You've a lovely figure, Elinor,' one of the other ladies remarked to Mrs Munroe.

'Thank you, my dear,' our new model said and assumed an expression and a position you might imagine for the Queen holding court.

The following week the upstaged model arrived to find Mr Faulkner already seated, nude, on the dais.

'Are you lot taking the mickey?' she asked.

Constable took her aside and, after some whispering and muttering, paid her. She went away without removing so much as her wristwatch.

There was a frivolous, end-of-term atmosphere in the room that day. We were a long time starting because Mr Clark kept on erupting with laughter and naturally we all joined in, which made it all the harder for him to stop.

'You must have been at those calinetics, Mr. Faulkner,' one of the old ladies joshed him.

'Now then,' Constable said at the end of that session. 'Who wants to do next week?'

I caught his attention first.

The intervening week was delicious. I smoothed over shirt after shirt with the iron, clearing a path before me as I thought of the liberation ahead. I dusted, polished, vacuumed, shunted a trolley round Sainsbury's with the alacrity of a five-year-old coming up to Christmas. I went to the garden section and bought a pirrus to put outside the kitchen window, and as I sank the trowel to plant it, I thought, This is me. I'm putting in something to grow here. And I set the little shrub into the hole I had dug, pushed soil around it and tamped it down.

At night—more than one night, anyway—I stood with my clothes off before the full-length mirror in the bathroom. I studied my body all over, every square inch. I looked face-on, sideways, over my shoulder. I searched for stretch marks, cellulite, bruising. I saw where the flesh maintained some vestige of youth and I acknowledged where it sagged, wrinkled and looked tired after the years it had sustained me. Each night I bathed in passion fruit oil, talcumed myself and rubbed moisturising cream into my hands and feet—all this in addition to my normal, daily ministrations to my face.

And when we sat at table, I regarded Matthew's thinning

69

hair and ballooning waist with contentment. I had conversations with him without ever being aware of a word either of us said. I smiled inwardly when he asked, 'Are you only having one potato?' I watched him fill his mouth with chocolate ice cream and wondered to myself, *When was the last time Matthew did something he had never done before?*

The excitement of emerging from behind the curtain bared to the world was wonderful. I padded across the linoleum tiles to the dais and adopted a position, my arms akimbo, my legs apart.

'Aren't you going to sit down, ak-chull-eh, Mrs Fraser?' Constable asked.

'No, I'm fine this way,' I replied. I felt ready to defy the whole world. The sense of emancipation was fantastically arousing. A smile I couldn't shake off played on my lips for the next two hours. Here I was, a thing of beauty, an object of desire, displayed for all to see.

Most of us had the chance to model twice before the end of the summer term. After that—no more. Constable took early retirement to concentrate on his painting and none of us returned in the autumn. The effect of the life class on me was total; it was as though weights had been lifted off me. Naturally, I left my husband.

PLAYING GERSHWIN

W HILE HEATHER COOKED dinner, Charlie watched a tape of the opening ceremony of the 1984 Olympic Games. An awful lot of pianists were playing *Rhapsody In Blue* on the screen. Even though it had been a long time since 1984, Charlie really loved to watch this tape.

Charlie and Heather sat down to dinner. It was still light outside; the clocks had recently come forward. There were several signs of spring in the garden, and in Charlie.

'I could really do with a change of job,' he said. 'Something exciting.'

'Somebody was advertising for a gunslinger in the *Guardian* today,' Heather said.

'They would be. Thursday is gunslingers' day in the *Guardian*.'

Charlie and Heather ate their cauliflower cheese.

'You're better sticking with what you've got,' Heather said. 'There's a good pension scheme.'

'Pension? I'm only just thirty!'

Heather didn't answer him, but continued, 'When are you going to paint the bathroom? You've been talking about it for ages.'

'I know,' Charlie said. He was already thinking about something else.

Outside in the garden, where he went for a little peace, Charlie pottered about with a hoe. A black cat he knew by sight sat on the gate pillar. Charlie nodded at it. The cat gave him a very odd look and floated to the footpath. Then a girl was standing there. She smiled.

'Hello,' said Charlie.

'Hi.' She had shiny red hair and, of course, freckles. 'Is that your cat?' she asked.

'No. I don't know whose cat that is. It's a weird cat, though. I know that much.' Charlie leaned on the hoe. He had a big nose, which the little girl was looking at. It was like an avocado, only it wasn't green.

'What's your name?' Charlie asked.

'Molly. I live at 62.' She pointed to the place. 'We just moved in at the weekend.'

Charlie thought Molly was all right but, really, he was thinking about something else. Or rather, he wasn't thinking about anything. He couldn't concentrate his mind. The next time he looked her way, Molly was gone.

In bed that night, with his wife and his electric blanket, Charlie thought how strange it was that they had ended up with an electric blanket. He remembered how much he and Heather had to say to each other in the past. Now they watched TV in the evenings. They watched game shows!

Charlie couldn't get to sleep and Heather was snoring. Carefully, he got out of bed and went downstairs. He boiled up the last of the milk, poured it into a mug and added a cinnamon stick. Charlie looked at his favourite hot drink and knew he would sleep.

He dreamed about a racoon. Nothing happened. The racoon didn't do much—just sat up a tree. It looked good, though. That racoon made Charlie feel better than he had for a long time. It was a good dream.

The milkman was late the next morning and Heather

wanted to know where all the milk had gone. Charlie told her. She gave him a look designed to fell a charging rhino economically, but then the milkman made his delivery. Charlie was staring out the window and his jaw had dropped. He resembled a little boy who, minutes after his best friend has convinced him that Santa Claus doesn't exist, sees Santa Claus.

'What is it?' Heather asked, puzzled.

'A racoon,' Charlie said.

The racoon wasn't friendly—in fact, any time Charlie or Heather went near, it acted like they weren't there. Charlie fed it monkey nuts and cabbage on an enamelled dish and didn't give it a name because it wasn't a pet. It was just 'The Racoon'.

'You're going to have to phone the zoo,' Heather said. 'This thing's obviously escaped.'

'There is no zoo in Manchester.'

He decided not to tell her what he had dreamt the night before.

Nearly home on his way back from work, Charlie ran into Molly. He told her to come with him.

'What is it?' Molly asked, looking up the tree in Charlie's back garden.

'It's a racoon.'

'What, like a racoon-skin cap?'

'Yes. I dreamt about it last night and this morning it was here. Funny, eh?'

On Saturday morning, Heather found Charlie in the bathroom. He had a paintbrush in his hand.

'What are you doing?'

Charlie looked at the paintbrush. 'Painting the bathroom.'

'What're all these lines on the wall?'

'I'm doing a mural,' Charlie said.

'Oh. What of?'

'Eighty pianists playing Gershwin's *Rhapsody In Blue*.'

There was a silence for a moment. 'How will anyone know what they're playing?'

'I'll tell 'em.'

The next day, they discovered that the racoon in the garden had gone. Charlie hoped, since it had been dreamt up, that it had simply disappeared. Then, on the six o'clock news, there was a report that a strange animal had been stealing eggs from a hen-house near Northenden. The farmer had never seen anything like it. The animal he'd seen running away put him in mind of a bear-cub.

'It was the wrong diet,' Charlie said. 'We drove him away.'

In bed one night later in the week, Charlie stirred his hot milk with a piece of cinnamon bark. Heather said the cinnamon looked disgusting. Charlie sipped from his mug contentedly. He dreamt he was walking through Southern Cemetery with a tiger on a lead. It was a very good-natured tiger. It would rub its head against Charlie's leg and knock him over. It was like the racoon dream—it made Charlie feel good.

'We're going to have to go to the butcher's today,' Charlie said to Heather at breakfast.

'But we're vegetarians.'

'We are. He's not,' Charlie said, pointing towards the tiger in the back garden.

Charlie spotted Molly as he was seeing the police officer out. He winked at her. When the officer was on his way, Charlie went over to say hello to Molly properly.

'Have you really got a tiger in your garden?' she asked.

'For the time being. Somebody from Chester Zoo's coming to pick it up. The rozzers tell me I may be fined for having a wild animal without a permit.'

'Rozzers?'

'You know—peelers, cops. The long arm of the law. I told the officer I dreamt it.'

Later, Heather told Charlie she thought he was up to something. 'So do the rozzers,' he replied.

When Charlie dreamt he was swimming in Chorlton Baths with an elephant, he knew what to expect the next morning.

'What do you think you're doing ?' Heather asked him when she saw it.

Charlie raised his eyebrows and tried to look helpless.

The police officer told Charlie he'd gone too far this time. Charlie pointed out that the only way he could have got an elephant into his back garden was by airlift.

'I wouldn't put it past you,' the officer said. 'You want to see a shrink, if you ask me.'

They used a helicopter to remove the elephant.

Heather said she was going home to her mother's and she probably wouldn't be back. Charlie felt quite excited at having the house all to himself. He did some work on the mural in the bathroom and then he pushed a hoe around a flowerbed in the front garden.

That's what he was doing when Molly came along.

'Did you see the opening ceremony of the 1984

Olympics?'

'No,' Molly said. 'I was only two in 1984.'

'There about eighty pianists playing Gershwin's *Rhapsody In Blue*. It was terrific.' Charlie's face took on a dreamy look. He could have been thinking of hot milk with a cinnamon stick.

'What's thingy in blue?'

'*Rhapsody In Blue*? It's a very good tune.'

Reports about Charlie's dreams began to appear in the press. He was interviewed on *The Nine O'Clock News*. Then a reporter from the *Sun* called Charlie up and offered him £10,000 for his story.

'Please,' Charlie said. 'I'm a *Guardian* reader.'

Nevertheless, the man from the *Sun* appeared at Charlie's front door and asked if he could post a photographer in the back garden during the night.

'No,' Charlie told him. 'Dreams are private. Now go away!'

Molly said Charlie had been right to turn down the £10,000.

'I offered to go topless on Page 3, though,' he told her.

That same week, Heather came back. 'I decided to spare you,' she said.

Charlie dreamt an orang-utan into the back garden. Looking at it the next morning, as it sat plumped on the small patch of lawn, he considered how nice it would be if his dreams could do him some good. What use was an orang-utan to anybody?

'Can't you sell these animals?' Heather asked.

'You can't put a price on dreams.' He was becoming a bit of an expert on the subject.

Charlie enjoyed watching the swell of the milk as it started to boil. He poured it into a mug and whisked a cinnamon stick through it. He was going to dream tonight and he was willing himself to dream an escape from Heather, electric blankets and game shows.

Next morning, when Heather awoke, she couldn't find Charlie anywhere. She never did. She assumed that he had done a disappearing trick, a Reginald Perrin. But to begin with, she told everyone that Charlie was with friends in Aberdeen. 'He just needed space.'

The truth was that nobody knew where Charlie had gone.

One of the first to ask about him was Molly. Heather invited her in and gave her orange squash. They talked about Charlie's dreams for a while.

'Can I use your toilet?' Molly eventually asked.

Up in the bathroom, she studied the mural Charlie had painted—all those pianists and pianos. She looked very carefully, which nobody had, and she noticed a man with a familiar avocado nose, seated at one of the pianos, playing Gershwin.

MUD

L YING LIKE SHE WAS with her back to the world and her
face in *The Montgomery Clift Story*—she's a sucker for any
old tosh about Hollywood—Amanda wasn't in as good a
position as me to study life on the beach. She didn't notice
everybody starting to coat their bodies in this black mud you
could dig out of the top of the beach where the sand banked
and she didn't notice this Arab who started giving some people a hand with sloshing on their mud. But I did.

It was three American girls I saw putting the mud on first.
I don't like Americans much, partly because I can't stand
Friends, so I was earwigging but trying not to look at them.
One of the Yanks asked what it was supposed to do to you.

'It's good for your skin,' another said, smacking her
thighs with the grey gunge. 'It makes it feel soft.'

Everybody in the water was floating on the surface with
their arms and legs stuck up out of the water, grinning like
it took talent. This ridiculous Italian bloke was holding a
magazine up in front of him as he sailed slowly by.

'Is very nice,' he chipped in. 'You will like. Let it dry in the
sun, then wash it off.'

The Americans kept smoothing the mud over their arms
and legs, and, delicately, around the rims of their bikini tops.

'It smells,' one of them said.

I watched the technique. You just dug a lump of mud out
of one of the hollows in the bank. You could do it with your
hands. You brought it down to the water's edge, and then all
you had to do was soak the cake of slime in Dead Sea water

78

and smooth it all over your body. I half-fancied doing it myself.

Of course, I was sick of Amanda before we even reached the Dead Sea. One of the things that gets me about Amanda is her figure, cause there's more of her than there is of me, and she knows it. When we first got to the Dead Sea, the way she was lying facedown on the sand got right up my nose. I mean, her buttocks were sitting up in her bikini pants like two honeydew melons. From behind, I look more like a plank. (From in front, too.) Another thing about Amanda that does my head in is the way she never notices anything. I mean, she thinks she's really sophisticated and obviously she thinks she's gorgeous, but she isn't very aware of what's going on around her—not at the best of times—so even if she hadn't been lying face-down with her nose in a book, she probably wouldn't have noticed this mud stuff anyway.

A lot of people were at it now and the more of them there were, the more I wanted to give it a go. This treatment works on the same kind of idea as mud face-packs. I mean, you could buy this stuff all packaged up in the shops there at the Dead Sea. I'd seen a stack of it at half price in a sale bin, so it obviously wasn't all that popular. AHABA FROM THE DEAD SEA, it says on the front of the box I brought home. There's a model on the front, much more neatly blacked-up than anyone on the beach could manage. Maybe it stops you getting old.

But the Arab—I first saw him with a shy, slightly plump woman in a golden yellow bikini.

'Where you from?' he asked her. His voice was low and throbbing. I suppose a hypnotist could use a voice like that. She told me where she was from, which I couldn't catch. When I say she was shy, what I really mean is she acted embarrassed the whole time he coated her flesh with mud. She fobbed him off, saying 'No' when he began to daub about her chest. At this stage, I hadn't got the gist of what he was up to. I mean, I thought he was just trying to chat up this woman in the yellow bikini; I didn't realise how wide his tastes went.

Another point of interest for me on that beach—I like to take in my surroundings—was these two Palestinian girls sitting up on the bank. I say 'Palestinian', but they just looked like what I understand by 'Palestinian'. I'm not sure what an actual Palestinian looks like. Whatever, they were perched up there, each of them reading a magazine, both fully dressed, both wearing long-sleeved white T-shirts. Only one of them was wearing blacked-out pebble glasses, but they both had straight black hair swept back and knotted at the neck. Maybe they were sisters. They were built like Olympic weightlifters. Not in an ugly way, though; they sat up there like black and white sculptures. I wouldn't have minded looking like those Palestinian girls. I've got a thing about how skinny I am.

'Oh, poor Monty,' Amanda was saying. 'He's buggered his face.'

I was looking at my legs. Pale poles. I really belong some place where everybody wants to look as white as possible. I mean, stroking comes much more naturally to me than tanning. I decided it was time for me to splodge on more Factor 58. As I oozed the cream out of the tube and massaged myself with it, I saw that the Arab had begun work on his next project. This guy wasn't choosy, I can tell you. She was fifty if she was a day. She had skin like the top of a rice pudding and acres of sagging, wrinkled flesh up the back of her thighs. She was from England, I know, because she had a voice like broken china. I think she was Jewish, too. I don't know what her getting felt up by an Arab did for the situation in the Middle East.

'Where you from?' he thrummed.

'Surrey,' she said, like maybe it was a favourite holiday destination for the whole of the Arab world.

He asked, 'Are you enjoying Israel?' To tell you the truth, he was a right little creep.

'Very much,' she said.

He told her he was from Jerusalem, but by this stage she'd had enough.

'Thank you, thank you, thank you,' she dismissed him, and waded out from the shore. He was left with the wetted black cake in his hand, hanging in the air.

On his own now, and black against the hills of Jordan behind, I studied him. He was one of those Arabs that look as much African as they do Arab. He was slight, but muscled with it, like he worked out. His shoulders were very square and he leaned back from his ankles. His entire figure seemed to taper away to his feet. He was a much better shape than my Steve.

'What a flippin' tit!' Amanda went.

This knocked me back a bit, because I thought she was talking about the Arab. Feeling sorry for Montgomery Clift hadn't lasted long.

'Reach us that, Sarah, willya?' she went, pointing. I passed her our two litre plastic bottle of fizzy mango juice. Amanda guzzled, dribbling from the sides of the bottle, and gasped when she took it from her mouth.

'Fancy a dip?' She sprang to her feet, looking like a Spaniel.

'Don't mind.'

We had a bit of a bob on the surface of the water again. We'd been in before; it wasn't bad so long as you didn't try anything ambitious, like swimming.

'How are you?' he greeted us when we got back to our feet at the water's edge. He stood near us, very exactly covered in mud himself, apart from a neat area across his shoulder blades he couldn't reach, and his face from the cheekbones up.

Amanda didn't meet his eyes. It was her he was looking at. She just stood there in her gingham bikini, like she was waiting for a bus or something, her boobs perfectly fitted left and right in the pockets of her bikini top.

'Where you from?'

'England,' Amanda told him, not friendly.

He asked her some other questions and each time the tone of her answers batted them into the ground. Another of the things I hate about Amanda is that blokes always single her out. Not me. Also, she's got more confidence than I have.

'What is that stuff?' she asked the Arab. Told you she never notices anything.

'It is Dead Sea mud. You try it. Very good for you skin.' He was such a creep.

Amanda looked at me and giggled. 'Where's it from, then?' Doh!

'I get you some,' he said. Amanda glanced at me and raised her eyebrows when he went to the mud bank. I avoided her. I wasn't giving her any encouragement. Instead, I looked at the Palestinian girls, settled on the bank like two totems. I was wondering what they thought of Amanda when they watched the Arab at work on her. The way he put that mud on Amanda's skin was one of the loveliest things I've ever seen. He smoothed it delicately over the whole of her body. His fingers never once stopped forming a beautiful shape.

It was like ballet. He flattened his hand along her calves;

he cupped it around her thighs and ran all the way up them. He lifted her elbows, one at a time, gently, and painted blackness beneath her upper arms. When he needed to, he stopped and splashed more water on the mud cake he was working from.

'On you face, too.'

'No. Here, I'll do it myself.' She accepted the mud from him. When she was finished, she asked him what she was supposed to do next.

'Just stay in the hot.' He sat on a rock by the water. She stood a couple of feet from him, face-on to the sun. I noticed how short her legs were from the knee down. I'd noticed it before.

He indicated a rock beside him. 'You sit here.'

'No, I'll stand,' Amanda said.

He asked her what her name was and she told him.

'I am Michael,' he went. 'I am from Jerusalem. I went to Catholic school.'

'Oh. I'm from Altrincham.' She looked at me and laughed again, but I still wasn't playing along. 'Manchester?' she explained. 'Man United?'

What was puzzling me was what this Arab was after. I mean, if he was trying to cop off, was he really not bothered if it was with a fifty-year-old or a twenty-year-old? That woman with the tissue-paper legs made me wonder if he wasn't some kind of rent boy. It gave me the shivers, just thinking about it. I was really glad it was Amanda he'd been squelching up with mud, and not me.

She just stood there with her face lifted to the sun. She was wearing all-black trainers, which made her look even squatter than she was. To be honest, I couldn't see any sign of the mud on her drying. When I looked back to our boy, he was gone, managing somehow to do a rough crawl and heading down-shore toward the showers. I wondered if he had given up on Amanda.

'What's his game, then?' I asked her.

'What do I care?'

She's so cool that girl. Somebody should stick her in *Vogue*. The Palestinian girls were watching us now. I watched them back. They didn't care.

Five minutes later, this low, smooth voice, purring, said, 'I tell you fortune.'

Amanda had been standing still, waiting for the mud to dry. Now she moved for the first time. She turned to face him and her lip curled. 'I don't think so,' she said and flounced off.

I helped myself to some more mango pop and looked directly at the Arab.

'Hi,' he said.

'Hi, ' I said back. He flashed the ball of mud that was left over in his hand. 'You want?' he said.

I gave him a big smile. 'If you like.'

Next morning, before we left, I ended up going back to the mini-market across the car park there, where you could get AHABA FROM THE DEAD SEA, reduced from 26 shekels to 13 a pack. The Palestinian girls from the previous day were sat beside the shop when I came out with my Ahaba and I gave them a little nod as I went past, but they didn't let on. I wasn't ever going to use my Ahaba; I was just buying it as a little memento of what happened there by the Dead Sea.

Steve once asked me how come I never opened 'that mud kit', as he put it. I just shrugged.

THE WALKING PLAN

'THERE'S A GIRL there fancies you,' Sponge cried. Billy glanced across, following the other boy's line of vision. It led him to not one but two girls: a pretty one smiling, a plain, box-faced one looking irked.

'Oh aye,' he responded, not convinced. He went on circling, as he had been before, on his bike, which allowed him to catch the smile still playing on the pretty one's face. Hubbard sniggered. Two more circles told Billy that she had pigtails, tanned skin and honey hair and then he was off into the distance.

'Chicken!' Sponge yelled after him.

Often enough, Billy had daydreamt of walking a beautiful girl through this park. He had a plan—not that he thought he would ever get to use it. Not really. At the moment, he was heading for the ultimate destination of his walking-a-girl-in-the-park plan. He was pretty sure he would tell the girl in question—if she ever materialised—about his most precious secret, The Word Box, where he kept all the juiciest-sounding words in the world. Maybe not right away, though. It could sound odd. The grand finale of The Walking Plan was here at the other end of the park, next to the assault course. There was a row of big, thick-trunked trees at the top of a large oblong of grass. There was a path that ran along the back of these trees, which, every evening about this time, was bathed in pale, gold light. As you stood there, the sun behind you threw long shadows across the grass from the big trees. In his imagination, he saw himself right there in the gold with the beautiful girl—maybe she would be this girl with honey hair. Finally, from the shadows of a rhododendron bush, Sponge and Hubbard had to be peering at them.

'Those two,' Sponge would be saying, 'must be having so much fun.' This was a crucial detail.

Back in reality, horseshoes clicking on tarmac meandered into Billy's mind, until he looked up and scanned the park for the mounted policeman he knew would be there. He'd spotted the officer on the horse twice before and always like this, from a good way off. All he could make out was the bell-tent shape of the figure in his draped cape on horseback, hundreds of yards across the grass. It unsettled him. Just the sound of the hooves clouded his mood a little. He didn't know why.

The moment passed. On an impulse, he sniffed one then the other armpit. What worried him most was the notion that if you smelt bad, you were probably the last person in the world who would notice it.

He lifted an arm for another, more frantic sniff.

'Fwaugh!' somebody said.

Billy span around, panicked.

'What a stink!' It was Carol-Ann Murray, who lived across the road from him.

'Oh, hi,' he said.

'Your face.'

'You gave me a shock.'

'You're telling me.'

'You shouldn't do that to people.'

'Who should I do it to, then?'

One of the things Billy thought about Carol-Ann was that she was strange. She even looked strange: for instance, she wore a big, old tweed jacket that must have been her Dad's, plus she had a rocker's quiff and nerdy, horn-rimmed glasses. She was two years older than Billy.

'Give us a sniff,' she said.

'Get lost!'

'What're you up to?'

'Nothing.'

'How come your bike's parked over there, then, and you're stood here in the middle of the trees smelling your armpits?'

Billy hesitated.

'You're weird,' she said.

He watched her go, a little sad. Too bad you couldn't say 'Yes' when a girl offered to sniff your armpits for you; it would be a sure-fire way to find out if you did have B.O.

He was in the Butcher-in-a-Suit's shop, queuing, next time he saw the girl with the honey hair. His pulse went Formula One. He could ask her out, couldn't he? Well, he *could*.

His Mum wanted loin chops—or was it lamb chops? He wasn't sure anymore. Whichever, he hated coming here, because the Butcher-in-a-Suit always embarrassed him. The Butcher-in-a-Suit was a loud red face and a sweep of black hair above the offending piece of tailoring. He had a big thing for himself.

'Come for a sausage, have you, cocker?' he'd said, more than once.

Billy had contemplated beating himself to death with a frozen turkey.

When The Honey Girl left, Billy followed her out onto the pavement. The air was fresh and sharp, a cool tonic after the smell of poultry, blood and sawdust. Ten yards away, The Honey Girl was setting off across the road. Billy was doubly relieved: he realised as she moved forward that it was impossible for him to go over and speak to her. Nothing in the whole history of his life had given him any preparation for doing something like that.

At home, his Dad was reading *Lacrosse Monthly*. His Dad wasn't just a cricket fan, bad enough, but also the only person in the entire world who knew what lacrosse was. Billy tried to keep his Dad's thing about lacrosse quiet. His Dad raised two wispy eyebrows over a front page that said, LACROSSE FEVER HITS FALKLANDS.

His Mum asked him for the chops and Billy put his hand over his eyes and groaned. And he had been feeling so good since his reprieve from asking The Honey Girl out.

The reprieve turned out to be nothing more than a stay of execution.

'Here y'are, Billy,' Sponge shouted. They were in the park. 'Ask her out, chicken.'

Billy turned around. It was The Honey Girl—of course —and her box-faced friend. He wasn't sure if his heart was sinking like an anchor or rising like a lift.

'D'you think he's handsome, love?' Sponge said.

Billy wanted to lift the grass and tug it over his head. The Honey Girl laughed. Swept up on a tidal wave of worry, he asked her, 'Would you like to do something on Saturday?'

'With you?'

'Yeah.'

'Okay.'

Hubbard's Mum helped out at Scouts on Friday nights. She was beautiful and always nice. Nothing like Hubbard. Billy was entranced by the careful way she peeled her sweater off. She removed it without disturbing a hair of her precious, moussed bob.

Billy's chest turned to twinkling crystal. This was the mysterious world of women that he might be entering on Saturday: lipstick and delicacy, beauty and softness, perfume like a soft wind lifting you a little off the ground. A touch of that world could make everything in his own right.

Hubbard's Mum was arranging her sweater over a chair now. Billy absorbed her blouse's every perfectly pressed fold, the fineness of her fingers straightening the lambswool. It was like all his favourite songs.

At teatime, Billy's Dad took up his series of occasional lectures on the Labour movement: 'Of course, many people accuse the contemporary Labour Party of diluting socialism, Billy. But in politics, as in everything else in the world, it's adapt or die, isn't it? You know about Darwinism, Billy, don't you?'

Billy looked up from his plate and smiled weakly. His father took this as a signal to continue: 'On an island called Galapagos, you can find giant turtles.'

Billy had stopped listening. 'Galapagos' was echoing around in his mind. Definitely one for The Word Box.

Billy was queuing in the Butcher-in-a-Suit's again. Up ahead, beyond a sickle-shaped old woman, he saw Carol-Ann Murray. The Butcher-in-a-Suit came out of the cold storage, his cheeks like crushed raspberries. Carol-Ann was being served at the counter.

The butcher's eyes oozed over her. 'You're getting to be a big girl, aren't you?'

'This place is full of rancid meat,' she said, staring into the butcher's florid face. Then she swept out of the shop like the Queen's Rolls Royce.

A bass drum pounded in Billy's heart.

On the bus into town for The Big Date, Billy was thinking with great excitement about The Honey Girl, The Walking Plan, The Word Box. Up above his head, there was a picture of himself and The Honey Girl. They were at the end of The Walking Plan. At the far side of the picture were Sponge and Hubbard, looking at them. Billy knew what his friends would be saying: 'Those two must be having so much fun.'

The Honey Girl, who was called Michelle, wasn't interested in The Walking Plan, but said she liked going round town. They met in McDonald's on Market Street. She found a table and he delivered their drinks and apple pie on a tray. Michelle requested a straw. Billy headed back to the counter.

'Can you get two?' she called after him.

'What do you want most in the whole wide world?' she asked, making suction-hose noises with her straws. 'I want a midi-system for me room. I've got a ghetto blaster, righ', but it's old and a midi system is—well, it does more. I'm getting money for me birthday. I'm gonna spend it on clothes, righ'. When's your birthday? Mine's in two weeks. You can't come though. All the invitations have gone out.'

Billy didn't want to come anyway. He knew about girls' birthday parties: he'd been to his cousin Natalie's one year and he'd had a bad time: the girls kept locking themselves in the bathroom and shrieking.

They went inside the Arndale. Billy didn't know why, but he felt impossible weights hanging from his shoulders. The fluorescent light, the crowds churning around him and shops, shops closing in. Also, Michelle was getting him down. She wasn't The Honey Girl. The Money Girl, more like.

'Anyway,' Michelle said, as they reached the big escalators, 'See you. Righ'?' She smiled with her mouth and was suddenly descending. She waved from the bottom of the escalator, flapping her fingers. He raised his hand in response. He could taste iron. The picture that had been above his head on the bus coming in was gone. The words, 'Those two must be having so much fun' clanked emptily in his ears.

Billy lay on his bed with his arms flopped out, so that he made a cross. He thought of Jesus and retracted his arms quickly. He sat up again. On his desk, he noticed, was a chocolate biscuit he had forgotten the day before. He fetched it and unwrapped it. He looked at the bared chocolate, then snapped it in half.

'Broken,' he said, 'like a wafer.'

Like one of those little wafer discs in church that the vicar called 'the host'.

Billy squatted by his bed, reached under and pulled out a green shoebox. At his desk, he wrote 'Wafer' on a piece of plain paper, cut it out and put it in The Word Box, where it joined 'Corrugated', 'Mallard', 'Solemn' and 'Galapagos'.

In the evening, when the sun was going down, Billy cycled along the two or three roads that took him to the park. He ducked in behind the trees, drew up in the middle of the assault course and dropped his bike by the parallel logs. Presently, he lowered himself backwards and hung by his legs from a crossbar. His flop of fringe dusted the dark earth below.

'I feel like a raisin, but I'm really a grape,' he chanted.

'Oh, I see,' a voice behind him said.

Billy twisted. All he could make out were long legs in

Reeboks and flowery culottes.

'Eh?' he said.

The legs, walking on the ceiling, came around to face him.

'Carol-Ann?'

'Billy?' she mocked. Up above, upside down, she was smiling. It looked funny the wrong way up. 'What you doing?'

'Oh, just—'

'—Hanging about,' she finished for him. He laughed, caught the crossbar with both hands and dropped his feet to the ground.

'Ever seen an Educational Psychologist?' she asked.

'Nope.' He saw she was wearing an R.E.M. T-shirt.

Carol-Ann shrugged and said, 'Want a fight?'

'Don't mind.'

He'd no sooner spoken than she had him by the neck, his cheek clamped to her ribcage. She smelt musty. He quite liked it. Then she was twisting him to the ground. She mounted his chest like it was a saddle. She grabbed his wrists and pinned him to the turf.

'Huh,' she said softly.

Then her laughter flowed and, in a moment, his, too. She released his arms and leaned back on her hips.

'What d'you want to do now?' she asked.

The horseshoes clopping felt pressingly close. He strained his head up to look for the mounted policeman. He got a surprise: it was a mounted policewoman. Less threatening. Maybe it had always been a policewoman. Maybe it had never been threatening.

'Don't know,' he said. He clasped his hands behind his head. He stared up at the sky and let his eyes un-focus. The sun was drowning on the horizon. The assault course was bathed in golden, drowsy light. He suddenly realised he was playing out the part he had imagined for himself in the grand finale of The Walking Plan, although really he hadn't planned this at all.

'Those two,' Billy thought, 'must be having so much fun.'

THE SECRET LIFE OF FRANK SINATRA

In the daytime, he worked in a sandwich shop downtown in Belfast. At night, mostly, he would be in some club, singing. 'Hello. I'm Frank Sinatra,' he would say when he came up to the microphone.

The first time he saw Anne was a busy lunchtime in January. There was the buzz of impatient people, the sounds of the electric till and Radio 1 and Samantha who worked beside him going, 'Who's next there?'

She seemed refreshingly uncertain to Frank when she asked, 'Is it me?' A touch of the young Audrey Hepburn there.

'She's mine,' he whispered to himself. His heart went tweet-tweet like a little bird. Somebody was playing hopscotch on his nervous system. 'Hallo, Princess!' Frank announced.

'Oh, hello,' she said.

She didn't seem sure of how to take Frank. It didn't get any easier.

'You'd be so nice to come home to,' he crooned. 'You'd be so nice by the fire. What a wonderful day for a sandwich.'

Frank always worked with backing tapes; he packed in the organ and drums combos years ago. He had unhealed wounds where organ and drums were concerned. Any song in the history of popular music became 'Feelings'. Including 'Johnny B. Goode'. It was hard to lay your hands on

94

half-decent backing tapes, but now and again he was able to get as close to the golden sound of Francis Albert as anyone without a twenty-five piece orchestra could.

Frank would tell you that two things separated him from greatness: he was born too late, and his agent was a clown right out of Chipperfield's Circus.

The agent, Billy, came in about this time with news. Jimmy Cricket wanted to see his act. And if he liked it, Frank would get the season at The Sandcastle in Blackpool. Which Jimmy, as it happened, was promoting himself.

Jimmy Cricket! A season in Blackpool! Frank spluttered. 'Somebody slap me,' he said. 'What did I do to deserve this?'

You could have sold Frank one of those Sinclair electric cars. Billy explained that good news travelled fast, that you didn't get to the top and stay there like Jimmy had if you hadn't always got your ear to the ground, that this was what made the big guys big. The whole season was up for grabs, on the same bill as *The Sunday Sport Page 3 Extravaganza* and Freddie Starr himself. With a band thrown in. Immediately, a thought bubble with a twenty-five-piece orchestra in it appeared above Frank's head. It was a beautiful thing to watch those elbows in the string section swoop.

'Negotiations proper,' Billy informed him, 'will begin after Jimmy has seen your act—on Thursday.'

'Thursday? Today's Monday!' Frank spat.

Come the night, no Jimmy Cricket. Be fair, Frank thought, flagging down a wrecked Toyota with cabbie-plates. Benefit of the doubt. Who knew what problems the man might have away from the public eye? Ulcers, weak back, the taxman. Not meant to be personal. Think of where you come on his list of priorities.

The most important thing in Frank Sinatra's life was romance. He loved to be in love. The longed-for look that showed she was interested, the soaring, sweeping Nelson Riddle arrangements in your chest, sleepless nights—the whole *shemozzle*. 'Call me Mr. Moonlight,' Frank would say. Put him in a trilby and an Italian suit in the pool of moody light beneath a street-lamp and it wouldn't have been any clearer.

She began to come in buy her lunch two or three days a week. She liked the note Frank put in with her sandwiches one day:

> *You make feel so young, you make me feel so Spring is sprung. Dance with me.*
>
> *Love,*
>
> *Frank (In the sandwich shop.)*

She replied by postcard. Posted postcard—through the mail and everything. What more could Ulster's Mr. Romance ask for?

Spring has sprung. It's March—does that explain it? her card said. *I've got two left feet. Love, Anne.*

The fifteen words on Anne's postcard underwent more in-depth analysis than the entire text of the Maastricht Treaty. Was she interested? Not interested, but very, very considerate? Curious? Winding him up? Or what?

After prolonged thought, it seemed to him that the fact she had written her address along the top suggested she was interested. They corresponded. Two postcards each brought them to the Ulster Museum.

They arranged to meet at two. At five past, Frank wanted to run away. He wanted to go home. He wouldn't have minded dying. 'Sorry I couldn't make our date,' he imagined writing. 'I died'.

Mostly they spoke about everything but what was on his mind. They got very serious about various paintings. Later, they talked about films. He asked if she had seen *Three Men And A Little Lady*, which was a trick question: it was his benchmark for poor taste.

'What if I had seen it then?' Anne asked.

'Well—black mark. But not as bad as liking Phil Collins.'

'I love Phil Collins.'

It turned out she worked in radio.

'What?' Frank said. 'On the radio?'

'A bit. Not very much. I present a World Music programme on Sunday nights. But I suppose you don't like World Music?'

Frank didn't even know what it was.

They saw one another a few times over the next few weeks. He learned she not only liked World Music, but played violin. They didn't touch. Then she was going to be away for a week, seeing her family in Scotland. She was standing on her doorstep and he was on the pavement. There was a certain amount of uncertainty. Finally, he said to her, 'Take a look at that moon up there'.

She did, and he kissed her. With his hands in his pockets, he kissed her and when she teetered backwards they almost landed on the carpet in her porch.

When Anne returned from Scotland, she had changed. The kiss, or perhaps the break, had cemented something in her. They were in a wine bar off the Dublin Road. A gypsy

fiddler played and Anne said he was useless. She handed
Frank the three postcards he had sent her.

'What?' Frank's wave of worry developed tidal tenden-
cies.

'Your postcards.'

He loved the way she said that: 'Postcards'.

'I've decided I want to do something about you. So, you
can have these back for a start. If we're going to do this, I
want everything to be genuine. All of it must be sincere.'

Frank didn't understand. 'It's very simple,' Anne told
him. 'I don't want the business. All the stuff you've done to
your other women, all the romantic stuff—don't do it to
me. Just be sincere. Don't do anything you've done before.
Don't give me the business. All right?'

This was a tall order. But, on the whole, Frank reflected,
the news was more good than bad.

Not giving Anne the business taxed Frank considerably. He
would think of her and get a rising sensation in his heart
—in normal times, cue for a postcard. Now he had to
restrain himself. It wasn't just difficult; he was convinced
it was unhealthy.

He would be walking through town on his lunch break
and find himself lingering outside a florist's. In the scarlet
carnations, he could see possibilities. The roses were how
he felt, the chrysanthemums surely more than even she
could resist.

But somehow he made himself walk on.

Anne told him it was a condition that needed treating.
That was all.

Easy for her to say. She was supposed to like the business. It was only natural. For goodness' sake, it was part of
being in love.

But Anne informed him that being in love was a pile of nonsense. It was a figment of the imagination, which soon wore off. 'The important thing is friendship,' she said. 'Be my friend.'

All of which got Frank down. What was the point of being in love with somebody if you couldn't be in love with them? Avoiding the business really was very hard. And then he stumbled on a troubling idea: maybe he was just somebody in love with the idea of being in love. Maybe he was incapable of having a mature relationship with a woman.

In the end, although Jimmy Cricket hadn't come to see Frank, he did send someone in his place. The gig was in a club up the Ravenhill Road. *Tonight! Live On Stage!* the poster in the foyer read. *Frank Sinnatra!* Sinnatra double *n* for legal reasons, although naturally Frank always thought of himself as single *n*.

Anne was in the audience. Frank sang 'Witchcraft', 'I've Got You Under My Skin', 'You Make Me feel So Young'—he believed it was his strongest number. Frank sang his heart out. When it came to the interval, there was Billy the agent, toting a dry Martini for Frank, but no sign of the man from Jimmy Cricket.

'So, where is he?' Frank asked, heart-sick. 'Couldn't he stay or what?'

Or what, as Billy explained. The man from Jimmy Cricket had said he was really looking for something more modern.

'What did he expect from a name like Frank Sinatra?' Frank asked. 'Punk rock?'

Frank couldn't help but think that, what with the embargo on romance and now Jimmy Cricket, Blackpool and the twenty-five-piece orchestra all going up in smoke, life was really extending the thumbs-down.

In the days that followed, he went into decline. Samantha in the shop told him he'd lost his sparkle. On the phone, Frank said to Anne that he couldn't see her at the moment. Two weeks passed without them meeting up. Then one day Anne decided to walk over to the shop in her lunch break.

Inside, it was busy and she stopped for a moment on the pavement. Through the big window, she could see Frank. He seemed listless; he looked to have lost weight. She remembered the way he had first greeted her in there. 'Hallo, princess!' Through that window, Frank cut a poignant figure. Anne felt very much affected by what she saw. He was a good man, she thought, and she felt attached to him. She believed that if there were anything she could do for him, she would. Then she realised there was. She pushed the shop door open and felt her heart lift, as if she were sweeping something out of her way.

'I came to tell you I've changed my mind,' Anne said. 'About the business.'

'You have?' Frank said.

'Yes. I have. The ban is off.'

There were whole mailboxes full of postcards. There were bunches of pinks, bouquets of tulips—even, once, an orchid corsage. There were candlelit dinners with Peggy Lee in the background, dancing in the moonlight to slinky Latin rhythms, lingering walks in the spring rain, slow evenings before a log fire.

Frank was beside himself. 'I'm beside myself,' he said.

And then there were strings: Anne started to accompany Frank and found she had a taste for performing. She liked dressing up, too. So there were two of them, a golden voice and a sweet violin.

As he sang 'I Get a Kick Out of You' during a gig at the Newtownards British Legion, Frank looked out at the rank of dour locals, glowering under a cloud of cigarette smoke, their faces like Lurgan spades. Two verses in, thanks to a gadget one of the engineers at work had fixed her up with, Anne launched bow over strings, her violin was multiplied, the Nelson Riddle Orchestra swooped from the P.A. and, in the twinkling of an eye, this dank vault was transformed into the Sands, Las Vegas.

In the spotlight, Frank laughed out loud and sang as he never had before. '*I get a kick every time I*—' he threw his hand in the air Al Jolson-style '—*see you standing there before me.*'

In the daytime, he worked in a sandwich shop downtown in Belfast. At night, mostly, he would be in some club, singing. With strings. The rest of the time, he loved some-body who loved him right back. Otherwise, what would have been the point in calling yourself Frank Sinatra?

AND IN THE WISPS OF PASSING CLOUDS

BOB LAMONT WAKES UP and finds himself splayed on the floor. For a moment, he wonders where he is, what time it is and why he is in this position, with his T-shirt pushed up to his armpits and his trousers bunched down round his ankles. But as he returns to consciousness, the answers to these questions come to him quickly enough.

He is on the floor of his living room, where the wall-length windows overlook Belfast, a view dominated by the yellow Goliath crane at Harland & Wolff. He is on his living room floor and it is the afternoon of his fiftieth birthday. That oak floor is terrific to look at, but hard as hell on his back, and the reason he is lying there rumpled, near-naked (like a character in one of the French films he loves) is—

'Coffee, Bob?'

He twists his neck towards the voice and realises before he sees her that it belongs to Hannah Shilton, his friend going back more than a dozen years, and now, it seems, not just his friend but also his fellow perpetrator in some kind of frightful mistake, a frightful mistake because although Bob is safely divorced, his ex-wife Eve has recently been working on repairing relations, so much so that there is talk of them entering joint counselling—talk, although on Bob's part no clear agreement.

'Ah, hi,' he says. And Hannah, he sees, is standing in the kitchen doorway wearing his blue reefer jacket over nothing much. Nothing is what covers her surprisingly tan legs. Tanning studios are one of the features of life in Holywood, which is where Hannah Shilton lives, and her butterscotch legs in autumn are one marker of the frightful mistake etc.

'Hi,' she replies. This simple word has never contained so many levels of meaning, mostly impenetrable, but at least one of them saying, Yes! That's what happened!

'Tea, in fact. Please, Hannah.' Does he normally use her name? Does using it suggest increased intimacy? Or, perhaps, increased self-consciousness? Tea, he thinks. He never drinks coffee and sees himself as a sort of evangelist for tea drinking. Tea, you see, is a proper drink. A quiet cup of tea relieves stress. The British Empire, let's face it, was built on drinking tea.

Before lunch today, Hannah arrived unexpectedly with a birthday card and a bottle of Bollinger. 'It's already chilled,' she said, 'so we should drink it.' A cold sweat breaks out as he imagines what Eve (Eve his no longer quite as ex- ex-wife as she once was) would make of the hard facts on what happened next. What was he doing having sex with an old friend?

'Bob?' Hannah calls from the kitchen. 'Haven't you got any de-caff?'

'Sorry.' He is considerate enough to keep coffee in the house, but not that considerate. 'Just the stuff with the fuel.'

A whimpering sound comes from the direction of his bedroom. He raises his legs in the air to pull his trousers up. He puts his bare feet on the floor with a slap and heaves his pelvis up so that he can yank his trousers the rest of the way. He gets to his feet (not as easy as it once was, even though he either runs or swims every day) and pulls his

T-shirt down over his spare tyre. The sound level of the whimpering is increasing. His back hurts.

'Okay,' he says. 'Okay.'

'I'm sorry?' Hannah says, emerging from the kitchen bearing two large mugs.

'Talking to Homer,' he replies. 'Excuse me one second.' He crosses the broad room and opens his bedroom door. As he goes in, Homer comes out, turns a hundred and eighty degrees and heads back to circle his ankles. Bob's dog is a black Labrador whose face is young and kind. Bob got him after his divorce from Eve came through, which is over three years ago, now that he thinks about it. And now that he thinks about Eve, he remembers that in the first place Hannah was Eve's friend. There's something about this that causes his adrenaline to flow, although he can't quite put his finger on it

'D'you want a shower, Hannah?' he shouts, and, turning, sees that she is on the big, yellow sofa, looking at him. In front of her, on the coffee table, two mugs sit like an invitation.

'No thanks,' she says. 'I'm going straight down to Esporta to work you out of my system on a cross-walker.'

'Very sensible,' he tells her and—damn!—it suddenly comes to him why it's worrying that Hannah and Eve are old friends. That is precisely how Eve might get the hard facts on what has happened here. But he can't imagine Hannah and Eve drinking Bailey's at the Crawfordsburn Inn, talking about the Atkins Diet or Delia Smith's chocolate torte, and Hannah suddenly going, Guess what? I humped Bob on his living room floor. Or maybe he can.

He tries to remember if what they did might be worth jeopardising a friendship for. The first impression that comes to mind is that it all happened very quickly. He can picture her body again, the bits of it he saw, and these images aren't hard to live with. This Esporta she mentioned is, he knows, some kind of health club, and, really, as he summons up her flat belly and taut arms, he would have to say that she is a pretty good advert for it.

While Bob has been thinking, Homer has been fussing about with Hannah. He walks across the floor, still in his bare feet, and sits down next to her. She is sitting with her legs folded beneath her. He looks at her and she gives him a conspiratorial smile (his co-perpetrator, his collaborator). She wears her wheat-blonde hair in a bob that ends at her jaw. She has dry, cushioned lips. She never wears any make-up, but really, for a woman of forty something, there isn't much in her face that needs disguising. Her eyes are the blue you see in willow-pattern china and her fine eyebrows float over them like a pair of seagull's wings. What's not to like?

'Nice birthday treat,' he says.

'Wasn't it?' Her voice is warm and woody, like the sound of a clarinet.

He drinks more tea and places his hand on her knee, which, like his feet, is still bare. Homer sets his head on her other knee. Bob and Hannah look at this, at each other and laugh.

She says, 'We're not starting a relationship or anything, are we?'

She's suggesting they aren't, but perhaps she's inviting him to contradict her. 'I don't know,' he says.

Ten minutes later, when Hannah Shilton has got into her Mini Cooper and driven off to her fitness club and Bob has had a shower and got dressed again, he opens the glass doors in the middle of the floor-to-ceiling windows, and walks out to his shallow but long balcony. He leans on the steel railing and looks at the view. Prickly hawthorn hedges run around the fields, almost silhouetted.

When he wakes in the morning, he pulls back his bedroom curtains just as something is blowing towards him. He realises it is a rust brown leaf. It swoops and dips and flies right at him, sticking at the last moment to the glass. He wonders if it might mean something.

Bob feels weary, and he thinks again what he has thought before about being fifty: things aren't as good as they used to be, but they're not as bad as they're going to get. Which is how he motivates himself to get out for a run, never mind how weary he feels.

In the kitchen after his shower, he washes down his herbal remedies (glucasomine sulphate, calcium supplement, ginkgo bilabo, cod liver oil) with orange juice and studies the benefits listed on the ginkgo bilabo bottle. Apparently, it enhances circulation to the brain, heart, limbs, ears and eyes and improves mental fuzziness and memory loss. It may reduce cardiovascular risks and is used in treating cerebral insufficiency, senile dementia and Alzheimer's disease. Perfect! he thinks, and, as he's eating his organic muesli, wonders if 'cerebral insufficiency' is a genuine medical condition, or just more herbal remedy bollocks.

He dresses and puts on his shoes. He sets to work on a series of paintings. On the face of it, the subject is a friend who models for him. He sketched and photographed her in a corner of his studio (a room) on a couple of Sunday afternoons, but the real focus of the seven canvases is the light in this corner, which the paintings study at different points in the day. He experiments with colours for crepuscular

light and enjoys himself pushing acrylic paint around with
a sturdy, square-cut brush he's particularly fond of at the
moment.

As he works, he keeps a bottle of water handy—keeps
it with him most of the time, really—because he has read
that water not only gives you energy, but also fills you up,
thus preventing snacking (and getting fatter). So he drinks
water throughout the day, but the need to snack appears
not to have been diminished by it.

By lunchtime he is in Rouge Café in Ballyhackamore,
having a bowl of French onion soup. Something makes him
look up and he sees Eve coming along towards him—Eve,
as she still is for some reason, Lamont.

'Your soup will be getting cold,' she says, standing over
him, her eyebrows, as they always are, set just a little raised
towards the middle, so that the first impression she gives
is of looking quizzical.

'Sit down,' he tells her, 'you're making me nervous.' It's
a quip he has used before, but this time it's true. Her presence today makes him very nervous and a curious, empty
feeling overwhelms him.

She primps her lightly curling hair—she claims not to
mind the grey in amongst the blonde—which she wears
pinned up at the back, but loosely so, giving her the air of
some Thomas Hardy heroine, fresh in and windblown from
the moor. The slight flush on her high-boned cheeks cor-
roborates that, but the truth is her hair always looks blown
by the wind and her cheeks are always softly pink.

'How was your birthday?' she asks. 'I've got a present for
you. If I'd known I was going to run into you, I'd have
brought it with me.'

'I told you not to bother. What brings you over this end
of town?' Eve lives in South Belfast, off the Lisburn Road.

'I'm having a day off. I'm meeting a friend here for lunch.'

'Someone I know?'

She smiles and the way her upper lip sits proud on the lower one, the Marie Antoinette position of the mole above her mouth, the way her long nose curves at the bridge, all give her a supercilious air. 'Yes. It's Hannah, as a matter of fact.' Is she teasing him? He mugs an expression of curiosity being satisfied.

Eve combs the fingers of one hand through the other and leans in closer. Her blue eyes have an insolent look he knows well, although he also knows that the insolence can, like the supercilious set of her mouth, be inadvertent. 'Have you thought any more about our counselling?' she asks.

'Mmm,' he says. Since she last mentioned it, counselling of any kind has rarely crossed his mind and he doesn't like her use of the word 'our'. To the best of his knowledge, they have not had joint possession of anything since they sold their home over three years ago.

'So you haven't.'

'Haven't what?'

'Given any thought to counselling.'

'No, I have,' he says. 'Thought about it.'

'And what were these thoughts?'

'Well—as you said, it could be helpful and it can't do any harm.' (Although it could have them at each other's throats before the first fifty-minute session was up.)

'Good. When can we start?'

'Ah—' Bob looks down and, noticing his spoon, decides that, in the circumstances, dipping it into his soup and taking a mouthful would be his best next move. Faced with what seems like compulsory counselling, he can suddenly bring to mind a great many things about Eve that he doesn't like, things which, let's face it, played a large part in their break-up.

'You do want to see if we can make a go of it again, don't you, Bob?'

He has soup around his lips now, he can feel it, and must look like a clown. 'Well—I think we should explore that possibility.'

Eve's eyelids clench and her mouth sets hard. The mole above it seems to grow and vibrate, a black mark against him now. That anger is no longer hidden. 'I don't know why I bother, honestly I don't. You'd rather stay up there in your barn, daubed in paint, immersed in your solitude like a brown bear in permanent hibernation.'

Bob is desperately thinking about what he can say to suggest that he is rock-solid with her, (as one, shoulder-to-shoulder like Blair with Bush on Iraq), on this counselling business, while at the same time not actually committing himself to anything. 'No,' he protests. 'You're misunderstanding what I'm saying.'

'Am I?' She smiles, but it's not the sort of smile that says I'm very fond of you; it's the sort of smile that says I'm going to torture you in ways of which Amnesty International would not approve. Stuck for a clear way through, Bob looks again to the table for rescue and finds a paper napkin, with which he wipes the soup from around his mouth.

Eve sighs, gives him her tolerant, more-in-sorrow look and says, 'Sometimes I think we're back to where we were four or five years ago.'

He thinks, No, much worse than that.

'I'm just disappointed, you know,' she tells him. 'That's all.'

'Hannah,' he says, startled, never so relieved to see any-one.

'Hello!' Hannah goes in much the way Ian Carmichael used to in 1950s films when he really meant What's going on here then? 'I didn't know Bob was joining us.'

'He's not,' Eve says, without looking at him. 'He's just going.'

Too bloody straight I am, Bob thinks.

'Ohhh,' Hannah purrs, in a way that suggests either gen-uine or playfully ironic disappointment.

'Yes,' Eve tells him. 'I want to hear all the gossip from Hannah, and I'll find out a lot more if you aren't present.'

Bob swallows hard. He looks up at Hannah, who twin-kles back at him out of the side of her eye in a way he doesn't much like.

At home, with Radio 3 on, he does some more work, break-ing around five. While making a pot of tea, his hackles rise as he thinks of the parental tone Eve used with him in the café: I don't know why I bother, honestly I don't. What on earth was he thinking of when he agreed, however tacitly, to the idea of entering counselling with her? Sometimes I think we're back to where we were four or five years ago. He could spit. Why would he—who would ever—give up his freedom and independence to endure any more con-versations like that? He must have been going soft in the head to give the notion of counselling the time of day. He puts the milk jug back and closes the fridge door—closes it on thoughts of Eve.

The doorbell rings. Humming the repetitive part of the Schubert that is playing on the radio, he almost dances down the stairs. He's feeling so good about the solitude, about the music, about what he has managed to achieve today that he almost isn't bothered by the interruption of this momentary idyll. He opens the door, sees that it is Eve and says hello. It's spooky that he has just been thinking about her. He notes that she is wearing a strange floppy hat made from angora and, almost simultaneously, takes in the look of thunder on her face, her unusually florid face. There are shadows under her eyes and her eyebrows are angrily bunched.

'You bastard!' she roars.

The silly hat makes it hard for him to take the fit of temper seriously. 'What?'

'Bastard,' she repeats, this time in quite a normal tone, and slaps him fast and heavy on the jaw with the palm of her hand.

'What?'

'I'm not having you making a fool of me, Bob Lamont.' She fixes him with a fiery look for a second or two, then turns and storms back to her car.

His cheek is stinging, throbbing really, and as he puts a hand up to rub it, he mutters to himself, 'Who are you having making a fool out of you, then?'

Now Eve has turned and is coming back towards him. He wonders if she has heard his muttering. Her eyes are blazing.

'What?' he insists.

Her mouth is clenched and twisted as she swings her arm again and this time connects to his face with a fist. It hurts, but he doesn't cry out. (Why didn't I move? he wonders.) Then it stings and he touches his cheekbone and looks at his fingers and sees blood. Her rings must have cut him. Amazingly, she is still standing there. She's a good-looking woman, but nobody livid looks attractive. He knows as soon as he thinks of it that he shouldn't say it, but it's too late, he already has:

'Hey look — shall we just forget about the counselling then?'

A spasm ripples through her face muscles and she kicks him with some force in the shin. It hurts and immediately starts to hurt even more. He hops on his good leg and then, watching her leave (really leave this time), he falls over. He realises it's raining. Rain, wet rain, is falling on his head and the flagstone upon which he lies.

Upstairs, Bob snaps off the radio. Perfectly ordered Schubert no longer tallies with his mood. He hobbles to the bathroom and gets his meagre medical supplies out of the cabinet. He puts a dab of Savlon on the cut and covers it with a plaster. In the kitchen, he sits down with some ice-cubes and a tea towel and presses the pack against his bruised shin. He stays that way for a few moments, until a stiff drink comes to seem a good idea and he hops around the kitchen fetching the bottle of Jack Daniels and a glass. Back in his chair, he sips the smoky heat and feels no better. The phone rings. The kitchen phone is wall-mounted, so he has to get to his feet (foot) to answer it.

'Hello?' he says, perhaps a little more warily than he usually would.

— Bob, it's Hannah.

'Hi.' He tries to put more enthusiasm into this than he feels.

— Look, I have to tell you —

'What is it?' he asks, although he knows, he knows.

— I told Eve about us — you know, on your birthday.

He admires the way she has cut to the chase. No This happened, that happened; just the one salient fact. 'Did you?'

— One glass too many over lunch, of course. I'm really

sorry. But the important thing—why I rang, really—is that she's on the warpath, and if I were you, I would stay clear big time. Please.

'I'll do my best.' Balancing on his one good leg, he is growing tired.

—I mean, I know Eve's prone to being angry, but I've never seen anger like this before.

I'm not sure I have either, he thinks. 'Really.'

—You will be careful, won't you?

He desperately wants to sit down now. 'I will.'

—Are you okay, Bob?

'I'm fine.'

—Your voice sounds . . . strained.

So's my bloody leg. 'Really. I'm fine.'

—I'm so sorry, Bob. I've dropped you right in it.'

'No. Don't worry about it. She would have found out eventually.' How? If you hadn't told her, I definitely wouldn't have.

—Would she? Yes, I suppose she would.

He notices that Hannah's voice has brightened considerably in this last response, and he hopes he hasn't committed himself to anything.

—Anyway. That was it. Just wanted to warn you. And apologise.

'No need. I'll see you soon.'

—Yes, see you soon.

As he hangs up, he is aware of his lips tightening together glumly.

In the early evening, he drinks another Jack Daniels, which softens his mood. He remembers the film that arrived the day before from Amazon DVD Rental, loads the disc in the DVD player and settles back to enjoy one of his favourite films, *Baisers Volés*. The song playing over the title sequence stirs his heart (his tipsy heart) and he wonders if it's Georges Brassens. He begins to tune into the lyrics, translated in the subtitles, which are about lost love. Before the end of the song, he stops the DVD and plays it again from the start. This time he sees that the song 'Que Reste-t-il de nos Amours?' is by Charles Trenet. This time, he reaches the end of the song, and the words stop him dead:

> And in the wisps of passing clouds
> Youth's vanished face.

The following day, he goes down to the Newtownards Road and taxes his car. He puts ads up in newsagents for a new tenant for the house he owns in Strandtown. He has the habit of using his digital camera to capture details of life and in recent weeks with the little Pentax on walks in Belfast, Holywood and Bangor, has been recording anything in his path that interests him: a poster in an appealingly pre-war style, advertising a Bluegrass gig; a neatly half-eaten apple; a guy about his age with a Mohican; a shop window display of archaic white bras with pockets like sacks; a statue of C.S. Lewis; an unlikely street sign (PRESLEY AVENUE); a bicycle frame locked to a lamp-post and stripped of wheels and saddle; a busking saxophonist; a magenta leaf; graffiti saying PEACE, LOVE AND PETROL BOMBS.

Today, in the turnaround area at the end of Massey Avenue where you park up for the grounds of Stormont, he finds a sticker he likes on the back window of a car: I ♥ THAI KICK BOXING. As he walks up the hill and past the statue of Sir Edward Carson, who has his right arm in the air and his fingers spread, (possibly in a hostile gesture to nationalists), Bob thinks about Hannah, and what happened with Eve. His thoughts wrestle with him, so he focuses his attention on something external instead, on Homer, his all-weather friend, who has simple desires and pleasures. Homer likes driving around in the car with Bob, going for walks by the sea or here at Stormont, gnawing at Trixie Chew Knots, having his belly tickled and, more than anything, Homer likes Bob.

He visits his practice nurse to get his flu vaccine. She asks him how long it has been since he had his prostate checked. Walking back to his car, he has another thought about what it means to be fifty: that at this age, happiness is finding your glasses when you've lost them.

Bob wakes up at seven on Saturday morning and it dawns on him that he has had enough of reflection. He has had enough of thinking about being fifty. He has reached a point when he knows that he has to act.

Hannah has two teenaged sons and there is no danger that she will have been woken up early, so he puts off the call as long as he can—until nine.

'Breakfast?' he says, when she picks up.

—Oh. But our anniversary was yesterday.

Bob can't think of a reply, and while he is trying, Hannah goes on:

—Would you like me to make you something?

'No. I'd like to take you out.'

—Anywhere in mind?

'You choose.'

—Panini's?

'I'll collect you in half an hour.'

—In your comedy car? Thanks, but I've got my reputation to think of. I'll meet you there. Half an hour, did you say?

'Yep.'

Hannah is already there when he walks into Panini's, sitting at one of the two-person tables opposite the deli counter. She has her head down in one of the café's newspapers. 'Hi,' he says.

She looks up and smiles. 'Hello.'

He sits down. 'How are you?'

'I'm fine. What about you?'

'I'm fifty.'

'I know. What happened to your cheek?'

'Oh.' He touches the plaster. 'Cut it on a branch when I was out running.' He picks up a menu and glances at it. 'The full works?'

'Not for me. I'd already had some toast and fruit when you rang. I was wondering when you would.'

'What?'

'Ring.'

'Oh.'

'Yes.'

'Well —'

'I'm glad you did.' She smiles again.

He feels pleased, boyishly pleased, and, embarrassed, he flags down a passing waitress and they put in their order. When the girl has gone, he dares to look at Hannah again, her fair hair freshly washed he thinks and he can see make-up today, scarlet lips and dark mascara. Under her fern green coat, she's wearing a silver grey linen shirt. She looks smart, all right. He wonders if this was how she appeared before he rang; surely at least the make-up represented an effort she has made on his behalf? The way the soft collar flops askew seems to say something about her — that she is relaxed, maybe, and confident, too. She is confident; if he were she and she were he, he would by now have asked why the phone-call has been over a week in coming. But she doesn't ask.

Their order comes: black coffee and cherry scone for her, toast and a pot of tea for him. He watches her slice the cherry scone in half. She spreads butter and then raspberry jam over the surface of the two scone halves. The jam is runny and, as she covers the scone perfectly with it, the seeds appear to swim around in the viscous, ruby fluid. She bites into it, her head turning to one side as it dips. She makes a small, satisfied moan and chews. She swallows, shuts her eyes and moans again.

'Fantastic,' she says, indistinctly.

'Good.'

So entranced has he been with Hannah's, he has forgotten his own breakfast. He butters his toast and spoons marmalade onto it, takes a bite and washes it down with a mouthful of good tea. He thinks of what she is that he is not: sunny, for one thing, an optimist for another. He thinks of what she has done that he has not: spent umpteen years parenting—spent even more years being married, for that matter. He wonders again about the prospect of being her man. It would put him in some sort of relationship with her boys and one of the things he thinks is missing from his life is fatherhood. At best, he would be a stepfather and would that be enough? It might, but the kind of experience of paternity he thinks he wants involves little kids, beings he can have a share in shaping. Also, he realises, he would like to have a daughter. He just would like to have children, any kind of children, he admits, but he sees in this moment that it would matter to him more never to have a daughter than not to have a son and heir (as they say).

'What actually made you ring?'

'Youth's vanished face.'

She breaks off from drinking her coffee. 'Sorry?'

'I'm just being daft. I suppose I rang because it was rude of me not to have sooner.'

'Was it?'

'I think so.'

'I could have rung you.'

'No, I think it was up to me. To say thanks for my birthday treat, if nothing else.'

'But you've been in shock ever since.'

'Actually—yes.'

Later, as he waits at the counter for the bill, he watches her browsing at Panini's long, stainless steel shelves of epicene fare: pasta that looks like miniature sculptures, dried mushrooms, pickled walnuts, mustard, jars of whole black truffles. Cellophane crackles as she picks up and examines packages. The waitress who took their order acknowledges his presence and quickly produces a bill. He reaches her a ten-pound note and looks back at Hannah. Her coat, he sees now, is cropped with curved hems and large buttons and it's warm looking. Beneath it she wears a grey knit mini-skirt over black woollen tights. She is the sharpest dressed woman in the place.

He moves over to the shelves and stands beside her. 'Buying anything?'

'Uh uh.' She turns and regards him, an irreverent sparkle in her blue eyes, the seagull's wings peaked. 'You've been wondering what might happen next.'

'Yes.'

She looks up at him, clearly trying to look down her nose, but he is six inches taller. 'What were you hoping would happen next?'

Bob inhales air for inspiration and flares his eyes. 'Breakfast?'

A smile, like the sun coming out, spreads across her face. 'This has all worked out really well for you, hasn't it?'

ACKNOWLEDGEMENTS

'The Life Class', 'The Secret Life of Frank Sinatra' and 'Carcasses' were originally broadcast in the *Afternoon Reading* on BBC Radio 4. 'Carcasses' was also anthologised in *Northern Stories 5* (Arc Publications). 'The Only Living Boy' was originally published in *Parameter*. 'Playing Gershwin' was originally published in an illustrated, limited edition by The Incline Press, Oldham. 'Celebrity Blessings' was originally published in *Metropolitan*. 'The Urban Spacemen' was originally published in a slightly different form —as 'Why Men Play Bowls'—in *Tandem* (West Midlands Arts). 'Fruit or Vegetable' was originally published in the anthology *Pool 2* (Headland Press).

For encouragement and insight, I'm very grateful to: Julie Armstrong, Jenny Newman, Helen Newall and the writer's workshop I belong to: Nick Corder, Jan Freeman, Ursula Hurley, Heather Leach, Judy Kendall and Glyn White. I'd also like to thank my students, past and present, at Edge Hill University and MMU Cheshire, from whom I always learn a great deal.

I love my family! That's you, Rachel, Poppy, Noah and Maisy —centre of the known universe.

If this book is for anyone, it's for my mother, Margaret Graham, and my father, Bob Graham (1900-1963), who have done so much for me.

Jack Lloyd is responsible for the lovely cover image and I'm very grateful to him for letting it adorn this book. You can see more of Jack's work at the Creative Recycling Gallery, 40 Beech Road, Chorlton, Manchester, M21 9EL or on-line at http://www.houseofbystander.com

Lightning Source UK Ltd.
Milton Keynes UK
173203UK00001B/54/P